I0838670

The Stars within Series

Book 01

Stars Align

H. Winter

Copyright © H. Winter 2025

All Rights Reserved

No part of this publication may be reproduced, distributed, or transmitted in any form or by any means, including photocopying, recording, or other electronic or mechanical methods, without the author's prior written permission, except in the case of brief quotations embodied in critical reviews and certain other non-commercial uses permitted by copyright law. For permission requests, please get in touch with the author.

Table of Contents

Dedication

Kieran, my wonderful fiancé, thank you for putting up with me for 10 years ☺! And allowing me to read my nonsense to you at all hours of the day. Even when I don't even know what I'm talking about. Thank you for helping me build all my characters, storyline and world and thank you for getting confused all the time, with the amount of characters in the book, makes me giggle. Much love always xoxo.

Acknowledgment

To my best friends and family thank you for believing in me, this has been so much fun to write and thank you for listening to my ideas.

To Wren and Sasha, thank you for drawing the prettiest designs and making the interior look beautiful, I couldn't have done this without you.

To mum, thanks for reading through it a couple hundred times, and making sure my silly mistakes are minimal.

To Inez, thank you for helping through the drafts and making it more cohesive.

To Jemma, thank you for reading it through and helping with a very quick turnaround for development.

To Emily, thank you for reading it from an audience perspective and helping me build my world.

To the fans, thank you for picking up this book, it means a lot to me. ☺

May you always believe in yourselves and never give up on you.

Moon page breaks: credits to FreePik (Designed by Freepik.)

About the Author

H. Winter has enjoyed writing since she was little, creating fanfiction and fantasy stories that capture her imagination. She would often write with her dad typing, her first ever piece about the adventures of Kim Possible. As an adult she felt like she wanted to do more with writing; so combing her love for, dancing, singing, acting and cheerleading she became inspired to bring you the stars within series.

A note from H. Winter: I hope that this has rekindled some old favorites and imagination. I have loved writing this and all my inspirations and favourite things has made an appearance. Everyone should try to follow their dreams and don't ever worry what someone else says.

We are all imperfectly perfect, and we should always fly high and do our best to try.

Try is all we can ever ask of ourselves.

PART ONE

Prologue

Time counts down and days pass by, but everything leads to a set moment in time.

This moment may be short, but it is what you choose to do with it that counts.

Do you follow the path of light, of good? To protect others?

Or do you follow the path of darkness, of evil? To deceive others?

Or do you simply choose to balance it out, to walk the path of the in-between?

She shot up, her breathing heavy. Her skin was slick with sweat and her hair matted against her forehead. She gripped at the bedsheets before turning to stare around her room. It had been so long since a vision last came to her. She slowly shimmied her way out of bed and stood up shakily. She wrapped her arms around herself and hurried to the silver coat rack where her pink silk robe hung.

She slid into her robe and hurried out of her room, her footsteps echoing with each step she took down the long winding corridor. She pushed open a set of doors and stepped out onto the balcony. A cool gush of wind hit her and she shuddered. She stepped forward, the cold concrete beneath her bare feet, sending a shiver up her body as she gazed up at the night sky.

The sky was darker than usual on the full moon. She glanced around, the wind causing her long blonde hair to dance around her.

Exhaling sharply, she pulled the robe tightly around her, knowing there was not much time left. In the morning preparations must begin, for her world would no longer be in peace.

It was not instant. This war was a long time in the making. However, nothing could have predicted the disaster that followed. The glorious city of lights and colour was ablaze in flames. A shadow loomed over the city, drawing all the shimmering lights away.

The darkness had arrived. Its movement across the sky was slow and gradual, but the power it possessed was unimaginable. Slowly the stars fell one by one, until they were backed into a corner.

The sky went dark and she lowered her gaze in sadness. The time had finally come. She raised her golden crescent star staff above her and shut her eyes.

"Please… Be safe," she thought as the light exploded from her staff and a rainbow of colours shot up into the sky, disappearing into the atmosphere. She exhaled shakily and her staff disappeared in a puff of sparkles.

She opened her eyes and stared at a pair of cold black eyes against pale white skin. It grinned, showing off its white teeth before disappearing.

"You won't ever find them, and if you do, they will rise and protect everything the star's light touches."

She gave a heavy sigh as her body began to glow. It was time to go and find a place to slumber until the new stars aligned.

Chapter 1 Beginning

"Can you see me?" The Voice echoed in the light.

"Huh?"

"Can you hear me?" it asked again, the light flickering to darkness.

"What?"

"You'll find out soon enough." It all went black.

"Woah!" Her eyes widened as she felt her body drop. Her hand reached up and grabbed her top, her chest feeling tight as the hot feeling slowly disappeared. She shook her head and let go of her top as she glanced at her window, softly banging shut in the light breeze.

"What was that? A dream…?" She sighed, glancing at the clock. Her eyes focused on the little hand ticking before they widened in realisation.

"I'm late!" she exclaimed. She flung back the bed sheets and quickly jumped out of bed to find her new school uniform.

"I'm ready!" she yelled as she jumped down the last few stairs and swung round the banister, narrowly missing the full moving boxes.

"Good morning love!" a yell came from the kitchen. She entered the kitchen and frowned. A young brunette girl was swinging her legs back and forth whilst sitting on the countertop, a brown cardboard box next to her.

"Should she be doing that?" she asked, eyeing her sister as she headed towards the fridge.

"Brooklyn. If Kayleigh wants to sit here, she can." The shimmering voice of her mother beamed as she picked up the smaller girl. Brooklyn rolled her eyes before she sat down to eat her breakfast.

"Your father and I are out tonight, and Cal is working late. You need to look after Kayleigh please and pick her up from school. You also need to finish unpacking your boxes," her mother explained as she walked around with Kayleigh in her arms. Brooklyn put a spoonful of food in her mouth and nodded glumly. Brooklyn and her family had recently moved to Silver Valley. As a result, Brooklyn had been unable to compete in her equestrian competition and had not enjoyed her summer holidays.

"Mummy, can I be in charge?" Kayleigh asked hopefully. Her mother placed Kayleigh on the floor, tapped her nose lightly and smiled.

"You are always in charge, darling." She walked out of the kitchen and Kayleigh followed her mother.

"Mornin' all! I'm going to work now, hun. See you tonight everyone!" The loud thud from her father's feet could be heard as he hurried down the stairs. An embarrassed squeal came from Kayleigh, and a chuckle from her mother, which was followed by the door shutting.

Brooklyn slowly banged her head on the table, sighing dramatically. Every morning it was the same routine. Kayleigh was given the world, Brooklyn had to sort herself out, her mother was extra happy, her father was always in a rush and her brother was nowhere to be seen.

"They're always like this…" she sighed. She laid her head down and stared at the kitchen door.

"Oh Brooklyn…" Her mother appeared in the doorway, giving Brooklyn a wide-eyed look.

"You're going to be late." Brooklyn shot her head up and glanced at the clock. A shriek left her lips as she threw her plate into the sink and ran out of the kitchen, screaming in frustration as she went.

"I'm going now!" Brooklyn finally yelled as she clipped on her roller skates. She stood up and pushed off rolling down the road.

"Enjoy your first day Brooklyn!" her mother called happily. Her mother and younger sister stood by the door waving excitedly as they watched Brooklyn skating down the street. The two smiled at each other before heading back inside the house. The cobblestones shimmered slightly in the sunrays and the path was lined with a myriad of pink, red and orange cherry blossom and sweet gum trees. Autumn was looking rather reddish. The morning roads were quiet and most people Brooklyn saw were walking or riding bikes, and the occasional full commuter tram passed down the middle of the main routes.

On her journey Brooklyn still felt troubled by her dream which had been recurring since she moved to Silver Valley. Sighing heavily with the breeze chilling her as she skated along the street, soon enough Brooklyn made it to the large looming white gates of Silver Valley Prep. She rolled her way to the steps that lead to the main entrance before quickly taking off her roller skates.

The grounds were quiet. She glanced around, noting the trees blooming with cherry blossoms and the cobbled pathways that led to two different buildings. Brooklyn hurried up the steps and headed to the reception area. A woman was sat at the desk, flicking through a magazine.

Brooklyn inhaled deeply before clearing her throat.

"Hi there! I'm new here and I'm not sure where I'm meant to go?" she asked quickly. The woman glanced up and eyed her up and down before standing up and grabbing a folder.

"Did you enroll over summer?" she asked. Brooklyn gave a slight nod, hoping that was what her parents did. The woman flicked quickly through the folder until she came across Brooklyn's name.

"Brooklyn Catalina Toyama?" the lady asked. Brooklyn nodded, a blush forming on her cheeks.

"Uh, Brooke is fine..." The woman glanced at her before continuing to speak.

"Alright you'll need this..." The lady placed the file down and picked up a map of the school.

"This..." She ducked under the desk and picked up a folder with 'Silver Valley Prep' inscribed in silver floral patterns.

"And this..." She gave Brooklyn a pencil case emblazoned with 'Silver Valley'.

"And these." The lady gave Brooklyn a journal, a badge and a wallet folder.

"Here we like to make sure you are all equipped for the rest of your school life. If you have any questions don't hesitate to ask. We, at Silver Valley Prep, hope you feel welcomed." The woman sat back down at her desk. She passed Brooklyn an information pack and pointed to a door leading to the unknown.

"School finishes at four. After school activities are encouraged for all our students. We also offer a job service centre if you wish to apply. All contact information is in the welcome pack. Your first class is physical education; go to your locker and you'll find your school physical education kit. Enjoy." she said, eyeing Brooklyn. Brooklyn raised an eyebrow and headed to the door.

"Thanks..." She opened it and stared at the bright white hallway. She sighed and walked down, the door closing softly behind her. Brooklyn looked around. It was still silent as she headed around the corner leading towards a corridor of lockers. She glanced at her number and stopped. She placed her stuff in one hand and unlocked the locker with the other. She placed her book and her bag in and pulled out a sports kit. She glanced around her locker before closing it.

"Look out!" Her eyes widened as a body collided with hers. Brooklyn fell to the floor and grunted as a body fell on top of hers.

"Sorry about that!" a voice chirped. Brooklyn glanced at her lap and sprawled out across her was a girl with short brown hair and identical school uniform although wearing trousers and big red Doc Martens on her feet. The girl heaved herself off Brooklyn and held out her hand. Brooklyn took the smaller girl's hand.

"Thanks." Brooklyn said once she was on her feet. The girl nodded, smiling brightly.

"No worries!" the girl said. Brooklyn looked her up and down. She had very pale skin and bright wide brown eyes.

"Oh, hey you're new!" she remarked, "I haven't seen you around." Brooklyn felt her cheeks flush.

"Yeah, my name is Brooklyn Toyama," she announced. The girl took her hand and shook it.

"Nice to meet you, I'm Jia-Luli Guang. Call me Jia." She giggled at Brooklyn's confused expression as the two began to walk up the corridor.

"So uh, how come you were running like that?" Brooklyn asked. Jia glanced up at the ceiling and tapped her chin.

"Oh well you see… I was late getting up this morning! I had the weirdest dream ever, weirder than my normal dreams. I spent so long trying to work it out that I just forgot about the time," Jia explained.

"Oh, to the left." Jia pointed ahead, and the girls took a turn.

"Honestly, it's a good thing I ran into you, our sports teacher doesn't like tardy students but at least I have you as an excuse!" Jia giggled, and Brooklyn gave a small smile. "I'm not usually late."

"Must have been some dream," Brooklyn mused. Jia gave a thoughtful nod as she recalled her manic morning.

Chapter 2 Unexpected

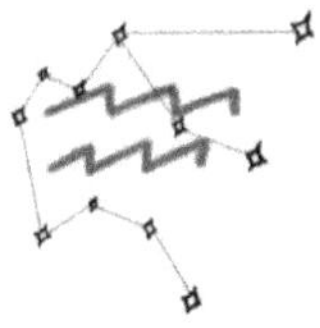

"Please, you must help."

The light shone brightly.

"Oh my! Okay… how?"

"Please… we don't have much time," the light said. All too quickly, the light flickered out.

"Hey, wait!"

Her eyes opened and she flailed her arms about, before realising where she was. She blinked a few times before stretching her arms above her head and yawning loudly, laying back down. She closed her eyes, but let out a squeal and shot back up when her alarm began beeping beside her. She slapped her hand across the alarm before jumping out of bed and heading over to her desk.

"I have to take notes on that dream," she declared to herself. She leant over her desk, turned on her radio and began bopping around her room. She twirled around, picking up bits and pieces for school before sitting down on her bed. She began making notes in her notebook about her dream as her head nodded to the music. Jia-Luli continued to doodle her thoughts about her dream until a loud thump on her door snapped her out of her thoughts. She dropped her pen and glanced at the door.

"Jia-Luli! You are going to be late for school."

Her mother's shrill voice rang through the door and Jia-Luli's eyes widened. She grabbed her alarm clock and gasped in shock, before jumping off the bed and grabbing her uniform. She was going to be late for school. She shimmied into her trousers and grabbed her clunky red Doc Martens.

"Sorry, sorry, sorry!" she yelled back. She could hear her mother's disapproving mutters, not only about her lateness, but in her native tongue, no less. Jia-Luli rolled her eyes as she headed into her bathroom, quickly brushing her teeth and hair before heading down the stairs. Slipping on the last step, she gave a squeal and landed with a thud. She rubbed her back and groaned softly, before jumping up and running into the kitchen. She grabbed her breakfast and flicked through her bag as she ate, suddenly realising she had forgotten her notebook.

She clambered back up the stairs and grabbed her notebook from her bed. She stared at the picture she had drawn, before shaking her head and placing it in her bag.

Once she bounded back downstairs she opened the front door.

"Baba, Mama, I'll see you tonight!" she called. She was met with two calls of "work hard and stay safe," before she dashed out the door and headed down the streets towards Silver Valley Prep.

She ran down the street, her breathing heavy as the sun beat down on her. She turned the corner and spotted the glistening white gates. She ran through the gates and bounded up the steps, pushing open the door to the reception.

"Good morning, Mona!" she yelled as she ran through. The receptionist, Mona, blinked and gave a small chuckle as the door shut behind the sprightly girl. Jia-Luli headed towards the lockers when something caught her eye. She turned her head briefly and frowned. Turning back whilst still running her eyes widened as she bumped into a student.

"So, that sums up my morning," Jia explained. Brooklyn smiled slightly as they came to a changing room. The door was darker than the corridors, but the image in the top centre glistened with a silver glitter tint to it.

"So, why'd you move here? And choose this school?" Jia asked as she pushed open the door and walked in. Brooklyn raised an eyebrow as the two placed down their belongings and began to get changed. Jia pursed her lips together and blushed.

"Not like this isn't a great school! Because it is awesome. The top school in fact, so really hard to get into, if you see what I mean," Jia rambled as she hopped from foot to foot waiting for Brooklyn to finish getting changed.

"No, I get that," Brooklyn answered. Silver Valley Prep had put her through different assessments before even shortlisting her. Her parents had thought that the school was amazing, just what Brooklyn needed after the move. They wanted her to do just as well as her brother, and hoped that Brooklyn's younger sister would also go to Silver Valley Prep.

"My parents really liked it here. So… I'm giving it a go," she added as Jia led them towards the gym. Jia smiled merrily and gestured towards the door in front of her.

"Well, you're here now!" Jia exclaimed happily as she pushed open the door. The class stopped. Brooklyn's eyes widened as she stared around. The gym had two basketball nets and bleachers covering both sides of the room. The gymnasium was also fully kitted out with a gymnastics setup, with each section having different students trying different apparatus.

Brooklyn's eyes sparkled in awe as she stared at the tumble track and the bars. She felt a nudge at her side, and she glanced at Jia, who smiled at her brightly.

"You look like a tourist! Do you like gymnastics?" she giggled, causing Brooklyn to blush. It was short lived, however, when a man started yelling.

"Miss Guang! You are late! What have I told you about being late?" a loud, wolf-like man yelled, storming forward. Jia bent forward, taking Brooklyn with her.

"I am so sorry, but Mr. Ashfell… I was showing our new classmate around," Jia explained loudly, earning the attention of the rest of the class. Brooklyn straightened up and untangled her arm from Jia's hold on her. The wolf-like man, Mr. Ashfell, was now towering over the two girls as he frowned at them both.

"I suppose that's an excuse. Very clever, Miss Guang, as always," he said, turning around to the stopped class. "Class, we have a new student…" He looked down at Brooklyn expectantly and she let out a small sigh.

"Her name is Brooklyn Toyama, Sir," Jia responded quickly, noticing Brooklyn had frozen.

"Brooklyn. Back to work," he announced, blowing a whistle. Mr. Ashfell turned his attention away from Jia and Brooklyn, heading towards a group of girls on the ropes. Jia smiled and took Brooklyn's hand, dragging her along.

"We should probably warm up. Come on, this way!" she said cheerily. Brooklyn glanced around, her shyness growing as a few of the girls were staring at her. They whispered softly until the teacher walked by and then went back to their apparatus. Jia dragged them to the bars and sat down, pretending to stretch.

"So, tell me about yourself, Brooke. I can call you that, right?" she asked, smiling. Brooklyn nodded in response as she jumped up onto the bars, swinging slowly back and forward.

"There's not much to say about me really. I have a mum and a dad and two siblings," she said, as she heaved herself up onto the bar. She rolled forward and around, before back up onto the bar. Jia nodded as her eyes skimmed around the gym, noticing a few eyes on the new girl. Jia smiled slightly and glanced back up at Brooklyn as she rolled around the bar twice.

"That's cool. I'm an only child. What's your siblings' names?" she asked. Brooklyn sat on the bar and stared down at Jia.

"Uh, Kayleigh is my younger sister, and Cal is my older brother," she answered, before swinging down and jumping onto the ground. Jia stood up and nodded. She was about to respond when a whistle sounded. The two headed over to join the class around their teacher.

"Alright, I want you in two lines behind the tumble track," he ordered. The class mumbled a little before moving. Once everyone was in place, Mr. Ashfell glanced around. "Who wants to roundoff first?" he asked. No one moved or spoke until a voice piped up.

"I'll go." Brooklyn and Jia glanced around to see a girl with long red hair and a slender body raising her hand. She glanced at Brooklyn before walking to the track. She stopped by the edge of the track before running forward. She brought her arms above her head, leaping from her feet twisting her torso sideways and onto her hands.

She brought her feet back down together on the other side, once again leaping into the air and fully rotating backwards this time, before finally landing onto the ground. The class cheered her roundoff back handspring in admiration as the girl gave a small smile and walked back to her friends.

"I said a roundoff, but that works too. As always, well-done Miss Anderson," Mr. Ashfell said gruffly, rubbing the back of his head. "Alright, can anyone else match Miss Anderson?"

He trailed off as a blur of brunette ran past him. Jia's eyes widened in surprise as the class gasped. Brooklyn leapt off her feet and onto her hands, matching the red head's roundoff back handspring. The class cheered in amazement. Brooklyn turned to the class and stared at Miss Anderson, who stared back, folding her arms over her chest.

"Alright, not bad," Mr. Ashfell muttered, eyeing Brooklyn. "Miss Toyama, I look forward to seeing you on the gymnastics team."

Brooklyn looked back at him and smiled slightly as Jia bounded over giving Brooklyn a bear hug.

"That was amazing!" she gushed as the class began to take it in turns doing round offs.

Brooklyn smiled.

"Thanks! I don't know what came over me! I just love tumbling," she said, her eyes becoming starry. Jia smiled back until a voice broke their cheerful chatter.

"Jia. Who's your friend?"

Chapter 3 Rivals

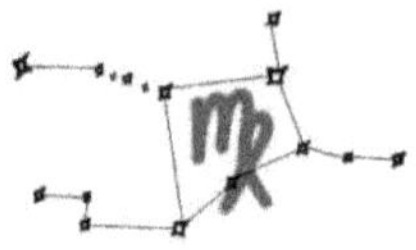

Jia and Brooklyn turned around to see the redhead standing tall in front of them, with her head slightly tilted to the side and her eyebrow raised. Now that she was closer, Brooklyn could see just how perfect she looked. Lola had long, silky, amber-coloured hair, with a fringe sitting diagonally to the left, tied in a high ponytail. She could be likened to a porcelain doll, with pale smooth skin and well-presented nails painted in a shimmering gel.

The silver sports top and blue leggings she wore hugged Lola tightly around her curves. Her eyes stood out to Brooklyn; for someone who looked quite stern and critical, Lola's hazel eyes were softer and more innocent than Brooklyn would have thought.

"Oh, hi Lola, this is Brooklyn. She's just started today," Jia explained. As Brooklyn nodded, she took a step forward and held out her hand.

"Hi, nice to meet you… Lola, right?" she began. Lola stared at Brooklyn's hand and folded her arms instead.

"Yes. Are you interested in joining the gymnastics team?" she asked. Brooklyn lowered her hand and stared up at the taller girl.

"Uh, I'm not sure, I've just started today… I think I want to get to know the school first before joining any teams," she answered. Lola raised her hand and flicked her ponytail over her shoulder.

"I see, have you done gymnastics before?" she asked, her voice almost sounding bored.

"All my life," Brooklyn replied, putting her hands on her hips. Lola hummed in response.

"Miss Toyama, Miss Anderson, let's see an aerial," the teacher snapped. Lola and Brooklyn glared at one another. Jia pursed her lips together and suppressed a giggle.

"I see you two are gonna become the best of friends," she whispered to herself as Brooklyn and Lola headed to the tumble track.

"Alright, first up?" Mr. Ashfell asked. Brooklyn ran forward and Lola's eyes widened in annoyance. Taking off on one foot, Brooklyn leapt into the air with her legs straight, rotating and twisting before landing back down, her feet facing the direction she just came from. She raised her arms in the air, displaying the end of the tumble with a proud smile on her face.

The class cheered in encouragement and Brooklyn moved off the track as Lola began hers. She did the same and landed gracefully, the class cheering louder for her as she walked off the track, smirking at Brooklyn as she went. Brooklyn frowned back as she stood next to Jia, who nudged her lightly.

"That was amazing, you should really join the team," Jia whispered to Brooklyn. The teacher returned to the class as Brooklyn stole a glance at Lola, who was staring straight back at her. Lola quickly turned back to the students talking to her.

"Thanks Jia… maybe I will," she answered. Once the teacher had finished talking, the bell rang, signalling the end of class, and the students headed out and back to the changing rooms. Lola flicked her long ponytail over her shoulder and sauntered her way back to the changing rooms. Jia and Brooklyn watched her go, giggling to one another before running after her.

Once Jia and Brooklyn were dressed, they headed to their next class. Jia bounded happily through the corridors, waving back at students as Brooklyn followed quietly beside her.

"So, here is the chemistry lab," Jia murmured, pushing open the door. Brooklyn nodded and followed Jia to two seats at the back of the room. Pulling out her science book, she explained

"Our teacher is quite lazy, so we'll be able to talk."

Brooklyn glanced around the class and spotted Lola; she was at the front in her clean blue uniform filing her nails. Brooklyn leant over to Jia.

"So, Lola-" She was cut off by Jia chuckling, nodding her head towards Lola.

"Lola is everything! She is popular, smart, one of the wealthiest kids in school. Her dad owns the mall, and her mum owns the docklands. Oh, and you can't forget how pretty she is as well." Jia grinned and Brooklyn raised an eyebrow, glancing back at Lola who was still staring at her nails.

"Fair enough," Brooklyn shrugged, as the teacher walked in. It wasn't long before the droning about chemical reactions by the teacher made both Brooklyn and Jia yawn. Jia leant down and grabbed her notebook, pulling it out of her bag and began to doodle as Brooklyn rolled her pen backward and forward on her desk. For her, it was only the second class, but she desperately wanted to go home.

Her body was tired, and her eyes were struggling to stay awake. She looked over at Jia and peered down to see her doodles. She was drawing swirling patterns surrounded by a starry night, and a circular shape was forming in the middle. Something was familiar to Brooklyn as she continued to stare at Jia's picture; she had seen it before, but where?

Brooklyn was about to ask when the door burst open and in walked a guy with spiky brown hair. He had a grey hoodie underneath his school blazer and red high-top trainers. His smile lit up the room and there was a cheeky glint in his eye.

"Sorry I'm late, I was helping at reception and lost track of time," he explained. The teacher glanced at him, a scowl ready, but it softened quickly. She waved a hand dismissively.

Brooklyn stared around the classroom; the girls were swooning. The boy thanked the teacher and headed to an empty seat next to Lola. She smiled at him, and he nodded back, smiling, before focusing on the rest of the lesson.

Brooklyn sighed and glanced back at Jia, only to find her staring back at her expectantly. Brooklyn frowned and Jia leant closer.

"I saw you staring, do you think he's cute?" Jia asked. Brooklyn rolled her eyes.

"I don't even know the guy."

"All the great romances start like that," Jia giggled quietly, adding, "and don't worry, you're not the only one." Brooklyn's eyes widened and slowly a smirk formed. Jia's eyes widened as she realised what she had said, and she waved her arms frantically.

"Oh, not me! Just every other girl!" She gulped awkwardly, causing Brooklyn to laugh. The teacher's head snapped around and her eyes narrowed at Jia.

"Jia, would you like to do the next experiment?" she asked. Brooklyn felt herself slump down in her seat as the class looked around. Jia whined before standing up and hurrying to the front of the class. The boy with brunette hair turned in his seat and met Brooklyn's eyes. She quickly glanced away, staring at Jia who was causing a loud scene but still completing the task with ease, much to the teacher's annoyance.

Once she was done, she trotted down through the tables and back to her seat. Brooklyn watched the class as a few whispered, eyeing Jia. She frowned slightly, before leaning over to Jia as soon as the teacher got back to her board.

"Are you super smart?" she whispered. Jia pursed her lips together and turned her head slightly, her body tensing a little.

"I suppose you could say that… I- I'm actually in the year below," Jia stammered;

Brooklyn's eyebrows rose in surprise.

"That's amazing Jia!" she gasped. Jia smiled and turned back to her doodles, her body relaxing.

"Thanks, though not many see it like that. They see me as an annoyance or a show-off," she explained, looking down at her doodles.

"Well, I think they're wrong. That's so good," Brooklyn said, giving her a cheeky smile and a thumbs up.

"Thanks Brooklyn," Jia breathed, her cheeks reddening slightly.

"That's something to be proud of. But you gotta promise not to make me look like an idiot," Brooklyn teased, causing Jia to giggle quietly.

"Oh, I'm sure you can do that all by yourself," she mused. The two girls chuckled quietly, finally getting to work on taking notes.

It was nearing the end of the day and Jia had spent most of the day showing Brooklyn around the school. Jia had enjoyed this very much, however Brooklyn was becoming overwhelmed, did everyone look like super models? Or model students? Brooklyn and Jia were on their last lesson. It was a free period and the two girls headed towards the library laughing and chatting with each other until Brooklyn dropped a few books on Jia's toe. Jia let out a squeal as Brooklyn laughed apologising as she bent down to pick them up but a hand reached out and picked up the book instead.

"You should be more careful." the low voice mused; Brooklyn looked up to find the brunette guy from earlier standing there with an slight smile on his lips. She blinked and stood up straight, holding out her hand as he gave the book back to her. He glanced at Jia and smiled.

"Ni hao, Jia." He said. Jia's eyes sparkled, and she nodded.

"S'up Tai!" She responded cheerfully, Tai, glanced at Brooklyn and her cheeks reddened. "Oh right, Tai this is Brooklyn. She's the new girl." Jia explained waving her hand around as Tai gave a nod and placed his hand on Brooklyn's shoulder.

"Hi…" she stuttered, earning a bigger smirk from Tai.

"Nice to meet you Brooklyn, see you around." He smiled at the two girls and turned, heading out of the library. The two girls watched him go and Jia cleared her throat and grabbed Brooklyn's arm.

"He's super nice. But come on!" Jia said laughing, causing Brooklyn to whine as Jia pulled her away, heading to a table to study.

Chapter 4 Threat

The final bell rang through the school and Jia yawned loudly as Brooklyn packed away her books.

"That was such a long day!" She exclaimed, Brooklyn rolled her eyes and pushed Jia back out of the library. The two walked along watching as students ran past, and others were chatting in the corridor. The two made it to the entrance.

"Well Brooklyn! Welcome to the school and I'll see you tomorrow." Jia said, waving to Brooklyn as she ran away from the school.

Brooklyn smiled. She had made her first friend and it really was not as bad as she thought it would be. She headed out of the school carrying her rollerblades and headed towards the elementary school. As she was walking, she spotted a long blonde-haired girl walking in front of her, she looked behind and frowned at Brooklyn but continued to walk.

Brooklyn pulled out her phone and began scrolling through her messages to check that her sister remembered that she was picking her up tonight. The girl in front of her looked behind again and picked up her pace.

The two turned in the same direction and Brooklyn was still absently texting her sister when she finally looked up. The elementary school, in comparison to the regal layout of her school, was colourful and bright. Even the gates were multicoloured. The blonde girl stamped her foot and turned to Brooklyn.

"Stop following me!" she yelled. Brooklyn's eyes widened, she slowly raised her finger and pointed to the gates.

"Uh. I'm actually picking up my sister." she explained. The girl's cheeks reddened and she scratched the top of her nose.

"Oh sorry! Just- can't be too careful you know." she stammered. Brooklyn walked towards her and the girl held out her hand. "Hello I'm Klara. I moved here last year. I'm still getting used to everything."

Brooklyn took her hand and nodded with a smile.

"Hi I'm Brooklyn. Just moved this week. Do you have younger siblings here?" she asked nodding to the gates. Klara shook her head and smiled a little.

"I live down this way, I pass here every day. I have two older sisters." she said. Brooklyn spotted her sister bounding along towards them with her 'two sizes too big' bag bouncing on her back.

"Hey Brooke!" Kayleigh yelled; Brooklyn rolled her eyes as Klara's eyes sparkled as she spotted Kayleigh.

"She's so cute!" Klara cooed, as she bent down to Kayleigh's height. Kayleigh's eyes narrowed as she stared Klara up and down before smiling brightly and putting her hands on her hips.

"Of course I'm cute! Hi I'm Kayleigh!" she said. Klara smiled and straightened up.

"Which way are you going?" she asked. Brooklyn smiled and pointed in the direction Klara was originally walking.

"That way, don't worry we're not following you." she mused. Klara chuckled, and the three girls began walking as Kayleigh talked about her amazing day at school, holding on to Klara's hand.

After a while Kayleigh had leant closer to her sister.

"I'm proud of you. You made a nice friend, mummy and daddy were worried you wouldn't make friends." Kayleigh whispered; Brooklyn's eyes narrowed before she looked down at her little sister. "But she's really pretty." Kayleigh commented.

"Wait, I can make friends." she huffed,

"No, you can't. Klara, I think you're pretty." she announced, Klara glanced at her and smiled brightly.

"Thank you, I think your sister is pretty cool." she said smiling as Kayleigh nodded.

"Klara, you sound funny, where are you from?"

"Kayleigh!" Brooklyn blurted, staring at her incredibly blunt sister. Klara laughed and kept walking,

"I said I moved here a year ago. I used to live in Sweden, I guess I haven't lost my accent. Do you like the accent?" Klara answered. Kayleigh nodded.

"It's pretty." she said. Brooklyn sighed and ran her hand through her hair, her stress levels rising because of her sister and her carefree attitude. Though Brooklyn was slightly grateful to Kayleigh. She had noticed the accent and did wonder where Klara was from. Kayleigh was also right, Klara was very pretty with long blonde wavy hair, bright blue eyes, sun-kissed skin. The school uniform complementing her very well. They carried on walking as Klara and Kayleigh bonded over their experiences of moving to a new school and city.

The streets had become very quiet as the three girls were walking and the skies were turning grey. Something felt off to Brooklyn as she looked around the streets, nothing was moving. The streets had lost their vibrancy as the girls continued to walk along. Brooklyn looked up at the trees, eyeing them suspiciously, the leaves hanging perfectly still with their orange hues seemingly duller than before.

As they continued to walk along the cobblestone path, Brooklyn realised what was wrong with this eerie silence. Their footsteps were falling silent! Kayleigh held onto the two girls tighter as they heard rustling.

"Do you hear that?" Brooklyn asked. Klara nodded.

"I don't remember this route taking so long to get home." she whispered as Kayleigh whimpered, Brooklyn shrugged out of her blazer and wrapped it around her sister's shoulders as they kept moving.

"Okay, Kay, I need you to trust your big sister, don't let go of Klara's hand." she said softly, smiling at her little sister. Kayleigh nodded and moved closer to Klara. Brooklyn turned her head, and her stomach tensed, suddenly wishing she had not looked. Skulking out of the shadows was a black, slimy, red eyed thing. Brooklyn shot her hands out and pushed Klara and Kayleigh into a run.

"Keep going, please and thank you!" Brooklyn ordered and the girls began to run. As Brooklyn glanced behind her, the creature was on all fours scrambling its way across the ground toward them. The monstrosity was vile, oozing black liquid as its four spider-like limbs dragged its bulbous body along the ground with the glowing red eyes in the centre of the mass fixed on the girls.

Brooklyn swallowed and turned her head as they ran around the corner and the three of them screamed as they collided into an imposing figure wearing the school uniform.

"Ow! Hey." the voice muttered, as Klara, Kayleigh and Brooklyn glanced up from the ground to see Tai frowning at them. "Brooklyn? What are you doing?" he asked, bending down and helping each of the girls up.

"We were being followed!" Klara exclaimed, gripping Tai's arm and shaking it. Kayleigh nodded as Brooklyn snapped out of her trance.

"We have to keep going." Klara added, Tai stepped through the girls and glanced around the corner. He stayed silent for a moment before turning back to the girls.

"There isn't anything there." he said. Each of the three girls poked their heads around the corner, there were people in the streets, and it was suddenly noisier again.

"But there was this weird black monster looking thing." a stunned Brooklyn muttered; Tai stared at her as Klara frowned.

"I couldn't see anything, but I could feel it…" Klara added confirming Brooklyn's theory, Tai raised his eyebrow.

"Maybe this was why Klara thought I was following her earlier." Brooklyn thought as Tai bent down to Kayleigh, who was whimpering quietly. He smiled softly at her and placed a hand on her head causing her to look at him with reddening cheeks.

"There is no need to worry, everything's fine." He reassured Kayleigh and glancing up at Klara and Brooklyn said "How about I take you ladies home?" He stood up and the girls nodded. "I'm Tai." He said, extending his hand to Klara who smiled.

"I'm Klara."

"I'm Kayleigh and Brooklyn's my big sister!" Kayleigh blurted as she walked forward, her arms extending up. Tai bent down and picked Kayleigh up.

"Alright, you first and then Brooklyn?" He directed his question to a nodding Klara. The group began to walk ahead as Brooklyn glanced back at the corner. Her eyes narrowing, before she followed the chatty girls, almost as if nothing had happened. The four went on, unaware that the shadow was still swirling and watching silently in the darkness before disappearing.

Chapter 5 Wonder

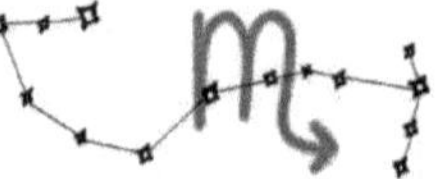

They had made it to a small block of flats. Brooklyn stared up at the light red bricks noting the small cracks streaking their way up. The building only went up three floors but staring up at it made it seem much taller, almost menacing. Brooklyn raised her eyebrow and glanced at Klara, her home didn't match her personality in the slightest.

"Thank you for walking me home." Klara said cheerfully as she raised her arms, wrapping them around Brooklyn and then Kayleigh and then Tai who chuckled and patted her back. Klara waved a little before running into the front door. Tai turned to Brooklyn.

"Okay let's get you two home." he announced and continued walking with Kayleigh in his arms.

"You know you don't have to carry her." Brooklyn whispered, eyeing her sister who poked her tongue out in response. Tai smirked.

"It's fine." he said, as Kayleigh began to babble on about her day to Tai, as Brooklyn silently walked beside them. She stared at him, her cheeks reddening. Tai stood out with his tall, muscular frame. His brown shaggy hair framed a face that was undeniably handsome, with chocolate brown eyes that seemed to hold endless depths. Tai gave Kayleigh a smile in response to her story. Brooklyn felt entranced; his warm smile could light up a room. Brooklyn wished she could be the one to make him smile like that. Her eyes widened at the thought and shook her head, pushing the embarrassing thoughts from her mind as they continued walking home.

After a short walk the three had arrived at Brooklyn and Kayleigh's new home; a modern looking four bed house, with cream coloured wooden pillars supporting the terrace above the front door. She inserted the key in the lock as Tai placed Kayleigh down on the ground.

"Thank you Tai!" Kayleigh giggled. Tai placed his hand on her head and smiled.

"You're very welcome. See you around." he said, as Kayleigh pushed open the door and threw her shoes off along with her bag before running up the stairs. Brooklyn pursed her lips together and frowned at her sister until she heard a low chuckle coming from Tai. She turned to him as he folded his arms over his chest.

"She seems sweet." He mused. Brooklyn rolled her eyes and shuffled awkwardly.

"I suppose. Thanks for carrying her. You didn't have to." she said,

"I have a younger sister, so I know what it's like." he said. Brooklyn stared at him for a moment as he took a deep breath and put his hands in his pockets. "Well, I'll see you at school tomorrow?" he added, aware that she was not much of a talker, and he took a step back and turned to walk down the path. Brooklyn snapped out of her thoughts.

"Thank you, Tai!" she responded quickly. He stopped and glanced back at her and smirked, nodding his head slightly before heading off down the street. She gave a small smile and felt a presence behind her.

"He's really handsome." Kayleigh called from halfway up the stairs, Brooklyn felt her cheeks redden before she turned into the house. Kayleigh squealed and ran back up the stairs as the door shut behind Brooklyn before she chased after her younger sister.

After spending some time entertaining her sister and sharing a easily made evening meal, Brooklyn flopped onto her bed and staring up at the ceiling she raised her arm and draped it over her forehead and closed her eyes.

"I didn't imagine it did I?" she whispered to herself, listening to her parents returning home and talking together. She bit into her lip, the clock on her bedside table ticking on as the wind blew softly. The moon shone brightly down as the stars flickered sharply. Brooklyn opened her eyes and pushed herself up, her brunette hair draping over her shoulder. She got out of bed and went to the window staring out of it, frowning slightly before shutting her window and closing the curtains.

Her room was enveloped in darkness apart from her lamp's dull light. She took off her clothes and slipped into her blue pyjama shorts and thin strapped white, with a pale pink cat face, pyjama top before climbing into bed. She switched off the lamp and rolled over, closing her eyes tightly.

"I know what I saw… there was something following us. But what was it?" she muttered before falling asleep.

Meanwhile, Jia sat at her desk, and scribbled into her notebook, the only light coming from her room was a flashing colourful lamp. She hummed and tapped her foot in time to the music as she continued to draw. The pencil scratched across the paper as the image slowly took form. She blinked a little at her work as she drew the dark body. She stopped suddenly and glanced toward the window, the wind causing the branch to tap lightly against it.

She inhaled and sighed quickly, dropped her pencil and got up to close the blinds. She turned to her bed and jumped on to it before snuggling under her covers. She sighed as she slowly closed her eyes, her thoughts on the dark creature she was drawing.

"I'm gonna be late!" Brooklyn screamed, darting down the stairs, dressing herself as she went and grabbing her school bag. Kayleigh giggled as she watched her sister run into the kitchen, grab the carton of orange juice and sloppily pour herself a glass.

"You know you really shouldn't go to bed late on a school night." Brooklyn's mother chastised, shaking her head softly as she watched Brooklyn hop from foot to foot as she made herself a slice of toast.

"I didn't." Brooklyn mumbled through a mouthful of the toast. Her mother sighed and continued helping Kayleigh get ready for school. Brooklyn hurried to her rollerblades and began to tie them up as her dad and older brother walked down the stairs.

"Shouldn't you have left by now?" her brother queried Brooklyn glanced up and scowled.

"Well, here's the funny thing Cal, I overslept. This is what happens when you do that." was Brooklyn's sarcastic reply. She huffed, causing her brother to laugh and ruffle her hair before picking up his car keys.

"I'll see you all tonight. Have a nice day Brooke." he called over his shoulder, as their parents waved goodbye to him. Brooklyn jumped up and grabbed her bag.

"See you later!" She called out as she jumped out of the door and sped down the road on her roller skates.

Jia was sat at her desk as Brooklyn arrived. She hurried to her seat next to Jia leaning over and peering at her drawing.

"Whatcha drawing today?" she asked. Jia hummed and glanced up at Brooklyn before turning her book around.

"I was drawing this last night." she began. Brooklyn peered closer at the drawing before her eyes widened and she stumbled back into the other table. Jia stood up to help her friend only to knock her notebook onto the floor.

"Brooklyn are you okay?" Jia asked frantically as Brooklyn stared with her mouth open at Jia.

"I saw that… that yesterday." she said pointing to the notebook on the floor. Jia frowned.

"How is that possible? I started drawing this last night." she explained, adding "I wasn't even sure what it was."

Brooklyn was about to respond when a familiar voice interrupted them.

"What are you two doing this time?"

They both turned around to face Lola, glowing in her uniform her hair down, flowing over one shoulder. Jia turned to her and smiled slightly.

"Nothing Lola. Just talking about my drawings." She chuckled; Lola raised her eyebrow unconvinced.

"Alright, well stop causing a scene. You're both really loud." she said softly, causing Brooklyn and Jia to look around to see the class whispering and glancing over every so often. Lola flicked her hair behind her shoulder and forced a perfect smile.

A hand reached down and picked up Jia's book. Lola, Brooklyn and Jia turned in unison to see Tai as he straightened next to

Brooklyn, who tensed slightly, cheeks flushing. He held open the book on the page of the drawing that had worried Brooklyn. Lola was next to him and her eyes travelled down to the picture, and Brooklyn swore both of their eyes widened ever so slightly before turning back to a poker face.

"Ni hao, Jia. You dropped this." he said, earning a smile from Jia.

"Sup Tai. Thanks Tai." Jia said, reaching forward and taking the book from him. Lola's eyes narrowed.

"Jia what is that?" she asked. Jia glanced at the drawing and shrugged her shoulders.

"I don't really know. It came to me in a dream, and I had to draw it, you know?" she replied as Tai folded his arms over his chest and Brooklyn glanced between the trio in front of her.

"How can we all be thinking about the same thing?" She asked, causing Lola to snap her head up and Tai to tense ever so slightly.

"I never said anything about thinking about that drawing. I was simply curious." Lola snapped; her eyes flickered to the door. "The teacher's here. Get to your seats." Lola pulled her hair back over her shoulder and strode passed Tai and Brooklyn. Tai glanced at Brooklyn and gave her a small smile.

"I don't get what it is either. But cool drawing Jia." he said before heading back to his seat. Jia and Brooklyn shuffled into their seats as Jia leant over to Brooklyn and whispered

"We gotta keep our voices down… but I think we're not the only two that have seen this."

Brooklyn nodded, her eyes on the back of Tai and Lola's heads.

"Yeah… weird." She mumbled as the teacher began to take the register.

Chapter 6 Appraisal

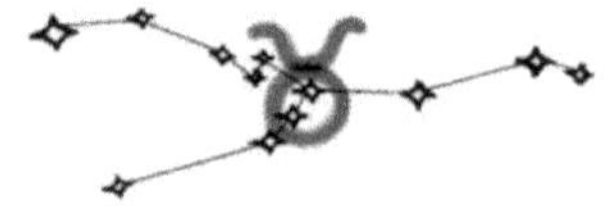

The day went by quickly and Brooklyn was helping pack away the supplies when she turned to Jia.

"You're not ready?" she asked. Jia shook her head, keeping her focus on her drawing. They had art last lesson and Brooklyn walked to stand behind Jia.

"I think I'm gonna stay a little while longer and keep working on this," she said, turning the picture toward Brooklyn.

"Alright then. See you tomorrow!" Brooklyn responded placing her hand on Jia's shoulder before heading out. Jia nodded absently and gently brushed along the outline of her creature.

After a few hours, Jia decided to head home. Having packed up her things and headed out of the school grounds, Jia walked along the road and stopped at the lights. She sighed and stared up at the cloudy sky, wishing there was more excitement in her life.

A car raced by and the lights turned red, she stepped onto the road and walked across, her short hair blowing across her face as she moved. Strolling along, kicking a pebble as she went, Jia turned down a side road and headed through the park. The trees blew softly, and the park was quiet. No one was playing in the park, the darkness slowly creeping through.

Jia glanced up at the trees, the once bright green leaves were fading to vibrant oranges, reds and yellows as fall was on its way. She shivered as the cold wind blowed and hurried her pace along, kicking the leaves up as she walked. The streetlights turned on and she stopped, frowning.

"It can't be that late?" she whispered to herself as she thought back to how long she had stayed after school, but the cleaners had not finished cleaning by the time she left. She heard a rustle, and as her heart leapt into her throat she glanced behind her, but nothing was there. Jia inhaled shakily and continued to walk until she heard a moan from behind her. Her eyes widened and she sprinted forward, slammed into the gates, pushed them open and ran along the quiet street.

"Where is everyone?" She thought to herself, running down the street until she turned into an alley way. She halted, a dead end. Jia gasped in annoyance and quickly glanced around to see some bins and quickly ducked behind them. Bringing her hands up and covering her mouth to muffle her heavy breathing she shut her eyes as she heard growling now, getting louder.

She opened her eyes and peeked her head around, her eyes widening in horror as the silence grew, the creature she had been drawing now in front of her with burning red eyes, slimy and slithering along.

She opened her mouth to scream but no sound came as the creature slithered closer. Grabbing the bin lid Jia swung forward smacking it clean in the face. Stumbling to her feet Jia ran around the creature and out the alleyway smacking into a tall guy with circular glasses, shaggy mousy hair and pale skin.

His hands were in his pockets with his body slightly hunched at his shoulders stood in front of her. His eyes widened at her panicked state but quickly softened back to boredom.

"You alright there?" he asked. Jia tried to speak, and the guy raised an eyebrow as she pointed down the alleyway. The guy stepped around Jia and looked down the alleyway and back to her.

"You know, it's not always safe being down alleyways, right? Where are you heading?" he asked. Jia shook her head and looked down the alleyway, her shoulder brushing against his forearm.

"Did I imagine it?" Jia thought as she glanced at the guy completely embarrassed. "Oh, I thought something was chasing me… I was trying to get home and got a little lost." she mumbled lamely.

"Right. I can walk you home if you want?" he said shrugging his shoulders. Jia nodded, and the guy raised his hand and gestured to start walking. She hurried to his side as the two walked towards her house.

The two had made it to the restaurant and the guy looked up at the sign, his eyes still bored.

"Thank you for walking me home… uh…" She tilted her head to the side and the guy looked down at her.

"My name is Xander. See you." He did not give her a second look as he headed off down the street. Jia stared after him before hurrying inside the restaurant and heading up to her room to message Brooklyn, she needed to see her as soon as possible.

Brooklyn was sitting in her room reading when her phone buzzed. She placed her book down, rolled over onto her stomach and grabbed her phone. She read the message and raised her eyebrow before messaging Jia back. She shuffled off her bed, picked up her socks and trainers and headed towards the stairs. When she reached the bottom of the stairs, she spotted her dad sitting watching the television, taking her hoodie she zipped it up and her dad held up his hand, causing Brooklyn to stop.

"Hi dad." she said, "What's up?"

"Where are you off to?" he asked, not taking his eyes off the television.

"I'm off to see Jia, she just messaged me." Brooklyn answered, her dad pausing the show and turning to face her.

"I'm really glad you're making friends Brooke, don't be out too late." He said with a smile. Brooklyn rolled her eyes and nodded and headed out the door, she quickly checked her messages for Jia's address before heading over.

Brooklyn had arrived at Silverian restaurant, and she frowned. In front of her was a relatively large building, but something was not quite right, it just looked like a house. It was two floors high with stepping stones leading to the front door. She walked forward and glanced around. "Am I at the right place?" she muttered, about to look at the address again when the door burst open and Jia appeared. Jia's frown instantly disappeared into a smile as she reached her hand out and grabbed Brooklyn's.

"Come on!" she said. Brooklyn nodded and allowed the smaller girl to drag her inside. Brooklyn stared around in awe, she was greeted by a beautiful reception room, with a small front desk, a large open leather folder on it. A beautiful crystal lampshade hung over head, illuminating the small room.

There were two closed doors on either side of her, one was clearly a bathroom and the other displayed a no entry sign. Straight ahead however was an open doorway with white curtains pulled to the sides. From where she was she could not see much but what she could see was beautiful. A small cosy restaurant that still had so much class, but the best part was the smell, a wonderful aroma of spices filling the building.

"You live here?" she asked, staring at the people chatting and eating their meals.

"Yeah. Mama! This is Brooklyn, she's a friend from school." Jia said as she suddenly stopped. Brooklyn turned around to come face to face with a woman with charcoal hair, tied up with chopsticks. Her face was paler than a porcelain doll and her lips were red as blood, and she had a calming yet fierce air around her.

"Uh, it's nice to meet you." Brooklyn said with a smile and the woman nodded at her.

"Hello Brooklyn, I am Mei Guang, Jia-Luli's mother." She spoke softly as Jia whined and began to drag Brooklyn towards a flight of stairs. Once they had made it upstairs, Jia closed her bedroom door, hurried to her bed and jumped on it. Brooklyn stared around as she smiled. Jia's room was a perfect illustration of her personality. There were papers and pens, paints and brushes, all strewn across the wooden floor; her wardrobe wide open with clothes pouring out of it. Funky lights danced as the wind blew in through the window.

A clock, paintings and pictures adorned the walls while her desk and bookshelf were covered in worldly books and artwork.

"So, what's up Jia?" Brooklyn asked as she hovered around the bookshelf. Jia crossed her legs and watched Brooklyn.

"Something weird happened to me!" she exclaimed. "I was on my way back from school, you know since I stayed late, and that creature I was drawing was real! And came after me! I ran, bumped into a guy and when I looked back the creature was gone." She babbled on. Brooklyn's eyes widened, she folded her arms and brought a hand up to her chin, deep in thought.

"I saw it too." She cut in. "When I walked home the other night with my sister and that girl, Klara. We bumped into Tai and it was gone." she mumbled; Jia sat up on her knees excitement radiating from her.

"What do you think this means?" she asked excitedly. Brooklyn shrugged her shoulders.

"It could be a coincidence. Or we're just really imaginative." she humoured.

"Well whatever it is, it's clearly scared of boys." They both looked at each other before laughing. Jia glanced out her window and her eyes widened as she bounced off her bed, startling Brooklyn.

"Brooke! Look! Look there!" she cried, jumping past the brunette-haired girl. Brooklyn followed her friend's gaze. There was a blinding white light in the distance.

"What is that?" Jia asked, they watched the light glow before sparkling into colours then quickly fading into darkness. Jia slapped Brooklyn on the arm and ran to the door.

"Come on, we should check it out. It could have the answers!" She gleefully squealed, as she grabbed her shoes. Brooklyn watched her before shrugging her shoulders and following quietly behind.

The outskirts of the city were dark and quiet, a thin stream of fog rolling in and the smell of salt air filled their noses as they walked slowly over the dewing planks on the dock.

"We shouldn't be doing this." Jia mused; Brooklyn frowned in confusion.

"What gave that away?" Brooklyn rolled her eyes and the two glanced around and tiptoed forward, looking for where the light had landed.

"What if it's a UFO? Or an alien? Or a meteor?" Jia babbled. Brooklyn's mouth opened and closed before she let out a sigh.

"You know UFO and aliens are the same thing, right?" she asked.

Jia turned to Brooklyn and tapped her nose.

"Or is that what they want you to think?" Jia continued babbling as Brooklyn squinted. She shot her arm out and grabbed Jia making her stop. The two were silent as they saw a blinding light burst around the sky, in the distance, before it completely disappeared.

Chapter 7 Time

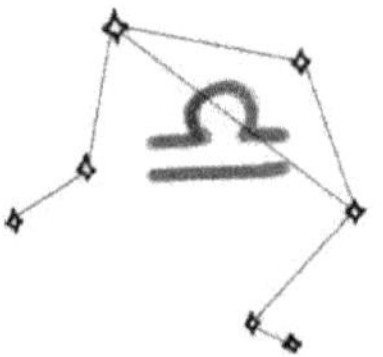

Brooklyn and Jia woke up with a start, they both were lying next to each other on Jia's bed. They were about to speak when they heard banging on the door and hushed chatter and glanced around the room both with identical looks of confusion on their faces.

"Jia-Luli! You are in trouble, is Brooklyn with you?" her father yelled. Jia scrambled over Brooklyn who yelped in surprise and the door was flung open. Both Jia's father and Brooklyn's father were stood next to each other, Brooklyn's dad taller than Jia's father and more rugged whereas Jia's father was in a smart male kimono.

"Brooklyn, I told you not to be out too late! Do you know how worried your mother and I were?" her dad asked, as Brooklyn rubbed the back of her neck.

"Sorry dad, I guess we…" She trailed off and glanced at Jia who gave her a sideways look.

"We were studying and got sleepy. It won't happen again." Brooklyn explained and her father sighed and turned to Jia's father.

"I'm so sorry about all this, Lei. No hard feelings, they are just teenagers after all." Brooklyn's dad said. Lei, Jia's father nodded in agreement.

"Very well, my apologies' Jim, our daughter can become quite forgetful. Jia-Luli say your goodbyes." Lei said, Jia nodded and gave Brooklyn a hug before letting go and they followed their fathers downstairs. Jim turned to Lei and they shook hands.

"Ah well, we look forward to having your daughter over, nice meeting you Lei. Come on Brooke." Jim said, and the two began walking back to their own home.

"So, what was that about kiddo?" Jim asked, Brooklyn looked up at him and shrugged her shoulders.

"We just got tired…" She responded quietly, and her dad gave her a look before wrapping his arm around her shoulder and squeezing her gently.

"Just please remember to message us, you know this is a new place for us too." he said. Brooklyn nodded.

"Yeah, I know."

"And I know you don't want to be here. So, running away does cross my mind. Like before Brooke." Brooklyn flinched at his words.

"Don't worry dad. It's not that bad." She answered. Jim sighed in relief.

"Well, that's good… Jia seems nice." he added.

"Yeah, she is." she nodded in agreement and the two fell into silence for the rest of the journey home.

Jia watched them leave before turning her gaze to the docklands.

"We were definitely at the docklands." she thought before turning in for the night.

A few days had passed since the incident and nothing out of the ordinary had happened to either girls. However one young amber haired girl was struggling. Lola was sat at her desk staring at her blank page. Every night for the past week, she had been having nightmares, dark yet colourful dreams.

With a voice calling to her and every time she tried to block it out it would scream louder. Lola sighed and heard laughter from the back of the room, turned her head slightly and frowned. Jia, child prodigy and Brooklyn, new girl, were having a pleasant conversation, laughing and smiling without a care in the world. Lola rolled her eyes and turned back to her page and began to write her name. Ever since that girl had arrived the nightmares seemed to have gotten worse.

She licked her bottom lip and pushed her hair behind her shoulder. The bell sounded and Lola hurried to pack her things and head to the one place in school that she loved. The worn down music room. She walked along the corridor until she came to a shabby old wooden door with a frost covered window.

Lola opened the door and her eyes widened in fear. Her eyes meeting a pair of yellow eyes, it blinked once before diving at her the creature screeching in her face. Lola slammed the door shut and took a step back. The door continued to shudder and creak under the pressure, and she waited until it stopped. Lola reached her hand out and opened the door. Nothing was there.

"L.A? What's wrong?"

Lola exhaled sharply and turned to see Tai standing there with his arms folded. She turned completely and pursed her lips together before clicking her tongue.

"What are you doing sneaking up on people Tai? And don't call me that." she huffed as he walked closer to her.

"Sorry but you were spacing. Come on it's a great nickname." he teased. She rolled her eyes and began to walk forward with him close beside her. "What's gotten you so worked up?" he asked. Lola sighed.

"That stupid drawing of Jia's." she responded quietly, trying to not look annoyed. Tai raised an eyebrow.

"I see. You've seen it too huh?" he mused. Lola stopped and faced him.

"I never-"

"I was only curious." Tai mimicked Lola and her eyes widened. "That's what you said to Jia, but I know you Lola, you saw it right?" he said. She lowered her gaze.

"I suppose I've seen it in a dream. But it's just coincidence." she answered. Tai observed her; she was nervous, as she pulled her hair back over her shoulder and started to plait it absentmindedly. "Don't read too much into it." She gave him a fake smile and walked off, her mind racing.

"Him too?" she thought, before she headed home for the day.

Tai watched Lola go. He sighed and turned his head to see Jia and Brooklyn running down the corridor, heading home for the day. He felt himself smile but stopped once Brooklyn disappeared around the corner. He began to walk in the opposite direction and towards the swimming centre.

"Hi Tai!"

"Good afternoon Tai!"

"Tai, how you doin?"

"Oh Tai it's so good to see you."

Tai smiled and waved where he could as he headed to the swimming pool. He stood at the edge of the pool and blew a whistle. He watched as the kids swam lengths and walked up and down the side keeping an eye on the slower swimmers. Tai loved his job; he loved the water and the freedom it made him feel. Every time he felt the water it would take him back to the holidays he spent with his family before they all started taking life too seriously.

He blew the whistle again and the kids one by one took a turn on the lower diving board, the ones struggling just hopping in and out of the water. Tai frowned; his mind partially somewhere else. He had not been one to be intuitive but with a cop for a dad and a doctor for a mother he noticed things more, intricate details of people, it's how he does so well in school and in work. Right now, his intuition was screaming at him; Lola and Jia and the drawing were revolving around the new girl, a flash of her entering his mind until he shook his head focusing back on the swimming lesson he was teaching.

The trouble was there was no trouble, nothing bad about her, no bad feeling, no gut feeling of doom, just pleasant curiosity.

"Help!"

Tai's eyes darted to the other side of the pool and without a second thought he ran round before diving into the pool. He swam quickly in the direction of a girl struggling to swim. He stopped in front of her and grabbed her arm, but she vigorously shook her head in her panic.

"Something's got my leg!" she screamed and went under. Tai dove under and grabbed the little girl's waist. His eyes fixed on Jia's creature. He kicked at it with all his might, forcing it to let go. The two broke the surface as the girl continued to cling to his neck, and he swam to the edge of the pool before propping her up on the side. Parents and other instructors ran over, comforting the girl as Tai checked her over for any injuries, before he glanced back at the water. His eyes narrowed as he spotted a dark shadow move across the bottom of the pool before disappearing. The little girl wrapped her arms around Tai's neck.

"Thank you." she whimpered; Tai patted her back gently his eyes never leaving the pool.

"No problem." he muttered. Everyone praising him for his quick actions faded into the back of his mind as he thought about the last few days.

Lola stood waiting for her friends when she spotted Jia and Brooklyn walking across the road. She sighed and turned away when she heard a car revving, turning her head her eyes widened.

"Watch out!"

In a matter of seconds Brooklyn saw the red car, shoved Jia to the side out of harm's way and closed her eyes as the car came speeding out of control towards her; the car never made impact. Yet her body collided with the ground.

Opening her eyes wide she stared up at Tai who was leaning over her. Looking back at the car, his eyes narrowed as Lola ran to help Jia up and pull her towards Tai and Brooklyn. The person in the car stepped out with a grin on her face. Her long legs extending her to her full towering height.

Her lithe body was adorned with deep crimson markings, her skin taking on a subtle purplish hue. She wore very little with her ragged black trousers torn off high at the thigh. Her midnight blue blouse equally worn with a large tear high on the chest.

Despite her disheveled appearance she still had a threatening presence. Around the four of them people were screaming as petrol poured from the car. In the next second the person had flicked her nail and suddenly the car exploded. The woman walked forward towards them, unfazed by the explosion, as Tai pulled Brooklyn to her feet, simultaneously pushing her behind him while Jia gripped Brooklyn's arm and Lola stood slightly in front of Jia.

"I wanted to meet you. At least once. It's a shame it's not all of you." The stranger said glancing around and placing a hand on her hip. "What a dump this place is. I don't know why mistress wants this. But no matter." She turned her attention back to the four, her grin widening, her red fiery hair floating around her.

"Who are you?" Tai demanded. The woman's mouth began to grow, further than any grin, her teeth sharpening.

"Mala. The bringer of nightmares. I am here to rip you from this world." She declared. Her hair stuck up like it had been hit by electricity and Lola let out a muffled scream as the woman began to pull on her mouth causing her face to turn into a grotesque monster. She lunged forward and Tai readied himself. A blast of light appeared suddenly between them and a woman, no older than forty, appeared.

"No." she said, and suddenly the four collapsed to the ground and everything went black.

Chapter 8 Shining

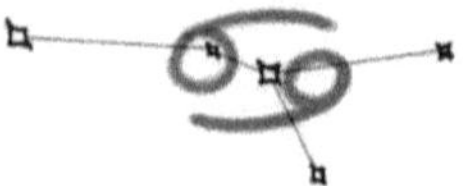

"No casualties. Just a fiery car crash and damage to the road and a few street signs, the fire department were called quickly."

Tai's eyes opened and he sat up, he could hear his parents in the other room.

"I'm just glad no one was hurt." his mother said, Tai slowly got up and made his way into the kitchen.

"Well, there will be an investigation. No one was in that car." his dad confirmed, flicking through his newspaper. His mother nodded as she continued to cook dinner. Tai stared at them both. They were calm and unfazed and his dad ran his hand through his brown, greying hair as he turned over the page in his newspaper. His mother focused on the cooking, her long black hair draping over one shoulder.

"And what time do you call this?" his dad teased as he spotted Tai, as his mother smiled at him.

"Did you have a nice nap?" she added, turning back to her food. Tai frowned.

"What time is it?" Tai asked, as he glanced around the kitchen.

"Nearly quarter to seven. Dinner will be ready on the hour." his mother answered and Tai raised an eyebrow.

"That can't be right it was ten to five, I was out." he muttered; his dad lowered his paper his own eyebrow rising ever so slightly.

"Well, when you go out with friends just be careful. There was a fire today." he said. Tai stared at his parents, his jaw dropping ever so slightly.

"I know I saw it." he said. His mother stopped cooking and the only sound was the bacon sizzling.

"You've been on that sofa for the last few hours." his dad said dismissively.

"So where are Maci and Charli and Eli?" Tai asked, his eyes narrowing,

"Eli is working overtime, but he'll be back for dinner and Maci and Charli have been upstairs all afternoon. Maci has an art project and Charli has been gaming with his friends." his mother explained.

"But I was there." Tai insisted. His mother walked towards him and pressed her hand against his forehead and brushed back his hair with her other hand.

"Are you working too hard?" she asked as he rolled his eyes and took a step back.

"I'm fine, I know what I saw." he repeated, "a woman stepped out of that car unharmed and went for Brook-" He trailed off and his dad turned to him.

"Son, remember you can't help others if you're not feeling your best." he said. Tai shook his head and headed for the door, grabbing his jacket from the banister.

"L.A. and the girls were there too." He muttered and headed out; his mother's eyes narrowed, annoyed.

"It's almost dinner!" she yelled, causing her husband to chuckle and go back to his newspaper.

Lola stared at the gem, which sat on her windowsill and shimmered with the sunlight. She stared at it a little longer before getting up and walking to her desk and sitting down, suddenly wishing she had never picked up the gem. She turned to it and picked it up. Ever since she picked up the gem, strange things have been happening to her and now she was waking up, when she knew she was somewhere else.

"Lola! Mum and dad are at business meetings, you need to make dinner for us!" A voice shouted from downstairs; Lola glared at the door before her eyes softened.

"Cass, I will cook a little later, I'm going out." She grabbed the gem and her jacket and headed out of her room and out of the front door.

Brooklyn woke up to see a woman sitting in darkness staring at a crystal ball.

"So, you finally wake up?" The woman said quietly. Brooklyn raised an eyebrow and glanced around nervously. "Don't worry I won't hurt you." she added. Brooklyn scoffed.

"That's usually what any psycho says." Brooklyn muttered as she shakily stood up. The corner of the woman's mouth turned up, but her eyes stayed expressionless.

"To each their own." she spoke.

"Who are you?"

"My name is Kumiko, and I'm here to help you." she said her eyes snapping to Brooklyn.

"Uh… what happened to my friends? And that woman?" Brooklyn walked cautiously towards the woman, but she stayed perfectly still.

"I suppose I can give you some help. As you appear to be the second in command." She turned back to the crystal ball.

"You're making no sense." Brooklyn said, Kumiko sighing.

"For now, I suggest you listen to your dreams, they will be your guide, start looking for those who have gems and..."

Brooklyn's eyes widened, and in a flash Kumiko had hold of Brooklyn's wrist and panic began to spread through Brooklyn.

"This." she said pulling back Brooklyn's blazer revealing a faint silver outline on her wrist. Brooklyn's eyes widened, and she let out a scream. Kumiko let go as Brooklyn turned her wrist over and rubbed it. It shimmered slightly, a silver hue glittering as she traced her fingers over it and the light reflected on it. As she rotated her wrist it appeared on the other side, she turned it back over, mesmerised by its beauty.

"What? What! What?!" Brooklyn shrieked snapping out of her trance. Kumiko sighed.

"It is your symbol it is what will help you find the others. Now go." she said. Brooklyn stared at the woman a little longer before running out of the door.

Whilst Brooklyn ran through the city, Jia stood in the restaurant kitchen, staring blankly at the food as she stirred the soup. She was confused. Completely and utterly confused. She heard some customers laughing in the other room and she sighed, she could have sworn she was out with Brooklyn, but now she was here in her restaurant, her parents yelling at her for not helping and she found herself making soup with no answers. She raised her hand holding the spoon and began pouring the soup into bowls.

"Ow!" Jia whined as some of the soup spilled onto her leg. She put the bowl down and bent to her leg to brush off the soup when she noticed it. On her calf just above her ankle. Eyes widening the spoon clattered to the floor as she dropped to the ground and brought her leg closer to her face, the mark shimmered, a light violet glitter was etched into the mark and her eyes were mesmerised.

"Where did you come from?" she asked curiously. It was beautiful, but it was not supposed to be there. And it was moving!

"Jia-Luli. What are you doing?" her father asked, Jia's eyes widened, and she lowered her trouser leg and spun around to face her dad.

"Nothing baba, can I be excused?" She began shuffling towards the door and bolted out of the room. Her father stared after his daughter before turning back to the soup, sighing and finishing off his daughter's job before his wife found out.

Brooklyn was staring at the cave at the docklands, her hand clutching her bag strap, eyes narrowing until she heard her name being called. She turned around and frowned when she spotted Jia sprinting towards her, her eyes widened, and she began waving her arms frantically.

"Jia slow down!" she squeaked; however, it was too late. Jia crashed, full force, into Brooklyn and they both fell to the ground. Brooklyn groaned as Jia sat up on Brooklyn and smiled sheepishly.

"Sorry Brooke." she chuckled; Brooklyn perched herself up on her elbows.

"It's okay, why are you here?"

"I dunno, I just remembered being with you on the road and that creepy lady and I wanted to come here." she babbled, Brooklyn nodding in understanding. Jia hopped up and pulled Brooklyn to her feet. As small as Jia was, she was quite strong Brooklyn noted. Brooklyn was about to speak when she heard footsteps.

"Jia, Brooklyn?" Lola questioned when she came to a stop in front of them, shaking her head.

"What are you doing here?" Brooklyn asked. Lola felt her cheeks redden and she glanced away, flicking her hair over her shoulder.

"… I was just going for a walk." She mumbled.

"Well, isn't this unexpected." another voice laughed. The three girls turned around to see Tai walking towards them.

"Tai!" Jia cried and bound over, giving him a hug. He chuckled and patted her head before looking over at Brooklyn and Lola.

"So, what brings you all here?" he asked, before folding his arms over his chest.

"Something amazing happened!" Jia exclaimed, "we think we saw Ufioh-" Jia was cut off with Brooklyn's hand clamped over her mouth.

"We don't know what we saw." she stammered, her cheeks reddening. Tai nodded and glanced at Lola.

"I saw a light, and thought, maybe tonight I would investigate-"

"You were at the docklands too?" Brooklyn cut in, thinking back to the first time she and Jia went to the docklands. Lola rolled her eyes and pulled her hair up into a ponytail.

"I was at a meeting with my mother. She owns the docklands." she explained. Jia glanced at Tai.

"Why were you here?"

"I went for a run." he answered, the three girls nodding as if it were the most obvious thing for Tai to do.

"We should have a look around?" Brooklyn suggested. Jia nodded enthusiastically, and Tai gave her a thumb up as Lola rolled her eyes but followed quietly behind.

The four unlikely friends began to make their way around the docklands until Lola stopped suddenly.

"L.A?" Tai said, stopping and turning to her.

"Let me just be clear. We saw a light, correct?" Lola said,

"UFO!" Jia smiled, Lola shook her head and Brooklyn and Tai nodded.

"Alright, in which direction did you see it? Otherwise, we're going round in circles." Lola stated.

"I don't really remember." Tai murmured. Brooklyn pointed to the cave where she had been previously standing.

"That cave, there is something weird about it. I think that's where Jia and I saw the light." she explained. Tai smiled and pulled out his phone switching the light on.

"It's actually a mining cave. These silver mines are actually why Silver Valley was founded in the first place." Jia corrected and Brooklyn nodded as Tai nudged Lola.

"I guess we're going exploring." he mused.

Lola sighed.

"Oh goodie." She huffed and the four headed into the dark entrance.

Chapter 9 Marked

Brooklyn, Jia, Tai and Lola were walking along the tunnel. It was quiet and eerie, each of them felt a pull, like they were being pulled further down, when they all froze to the sound of light scraping behind them. Lola, who was leading the way with Tai, turned around slowly and squinting into the darkness saw. In succession they all turned around causing Brooklyn's bag to scrape against one of the support beams. They all looked at her and gave a sigh of relief.

"Oh, it's not a monster." Jia pouted, earning a light smack from Lola. Brooklyn blushed slightly and glanced down at the ground in embarrassment, dust gently falling from the support beam overhead.

"Brooklyn, your bag moved." Tai said. Brooklyn frowned and opened her bag to see something shining and pulsing. She reached for it and pulled it out, her eyes glued to it as she held it in front of her.

"Pretty." Jia mumbled. Brooklyn nodded, it was a beautiful diamond, silver and clear.

"OH!" Jia yelped, causing the others to turn to her sharply. "I found one of those too! It was in my pocket after you and I had gone to the docklands the first time and I woke up in my room!" She explained pulling out a beautiful solid amethyst.

"Jia. You didn't think to question a giant gem in your pocket?" Brooklyn asked, Jia shook her head.

"Oh, for the love of…" Lola shook her head and turned away from the trio.

"Nope. I find lots of stuff in my pockets." She explained, smiling, reaching her hands into her pockets pulling out what she found. "See? Some staples, hair band, paintbrush, oh! Some gum."

Tai and Brooklyn exchanged bewildered glances as Jia ate the gum, causing Lola to gag.

"Oh and I have this!" Jia declared as she brought up her foot and there on her calf was a mark. Brooklyn's eyes widened, and she remembered what the woman told her. She shot out her arm and smiled at Jia.

"I have one too!" she exclaimed.

Jia's eyes sparkled and Tai smirked, however a scoff caused them all to look at Lola.

"This is stupid. There is no such thing as magic. Stop being a child." Lola snapped. Brooklyn glared back at her and they stepped closer together.

"Lola. It is literally happening in front of you." Brooklyn stated. Lola shook her head and folded her arms.

"This is some sort of trick. There is no way magic exists." she hissed. Jia and Tai exchanged looks as Brooklyn rolled her eyes and groaned loudly.

"Ever heard of seeing is believing? Because it's right in front of you!" Brooklyn shouted. Lola snorted, her hand absently going into her pocket.

"We've eaten some off food and now we're hallucinating." she shot back. Brooklyn let out a disbelieving groan.

"Are you serious?"

"This is stupid!" Lola yelled.

"Yes, it could be stupid! But guess what it is happening Lola, so start help…"

"Guys!" Tai and Jia shouted together, causing the two girls to stop and look at them.

Jia pointed to their hands and the two girls stared down and opened their palms as Tai and Jia held up their hands holding the gems. Lola, Tai, Jia, and Brooklyn were stood staring at each other, the gems they held in their hands were glowing, Brooklyn glanced at her wrist then Jia's leg which were shimmering, and she looked up to see a similar shimmer on Tai's forearm. The light began to grow and engulf the cave, Lola's eyes widened.

"Well damn."

After the light had faded, the four were sat on the ground, dazed. They looked around to see if anything had happened, but it was still them, with their gems and their shimmering marks.

"That was so cool!" Jia finally blurted out as she leant over Brooklyn's lap and prodded Tai. "What colour is your gem Tai?" She asked excitedly. Tai blinked and held up his hand revealing a brown looking gem.

"What is it?" he asked, looking at the girls.

"It's an Andalusite," Lola stated, before blushing and pushing her hair over her shoulder. "It's a rare gemstone. However, it can be rather beautiful on the right jewelry." she explained, glancing away.

"You seem to know a lot about them." Brooklyn said. Lola scowled at her.

"My father has to inspect all the stores at the mall, his favourite store happens to be the jewelery store. I happen to know a bit about them too." she huffed; Brooklyn stared at the stone a little longer before glancing up at Lola.

"What gemstone did you get?" she asked. Lola held up an emerald.

"Do you think that woman was here to stop us?" Jia asked.

"Maybe." Tai responded running his hand through his hair. Lola slipped her gem back in her pocket.

"For now we tell no one. Got it?" she said, eyeing Jia who smiled sheepishly. "We go home. Get some sleep, and we'll talk properly at the weekend." she instructed. The four stood up and Brooklyn pursed her lips together as the other three were chatting quietly about their newfound gems.

"Do I tell them?" she thought to herself. Ever since she met Kumiko, Brooklyn thought the whole ordeal had been a dream, but now as she felt the weight of the gem in her pocket she knew this was real.

"Lola, what do you think this all means?" Jia asked.

Tai placed his finger under his chin and folded his arms. Lola gave a small shrug of her shoulders.

"We don't even know why we have these. Or what it has done. But I agree with L.A. We talk more another time."

Lola let out an annoyed huff as Brooklyn cleared her throat and they looked at her.

"I think there is someone who knows about this. But I don't know how to find her." she explained. Jia tilted her head to the side.

"Well, it's all we've got so let's find this mystery woman." Tai said giving Brooklyn a smile.

"Yeah!"

"Fine. But we look at the weekend, it's late." Lola said begrudgingly and the four of them made it back up the tunnel, quietly lost in their own little worlds.

Brooklyn flopped onto her bed and groaned after the group had dispersed. She had headed home, was grilled by her parents for being out so late again and was now tired. Brooklyn reached her hand into her bag and pulled the gem out, starring at it until her eyes became heavy and she fell into a deep dreamless sleep.

Chapter 10 Altair

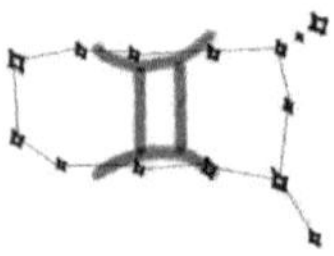

The weekend arrived, and Brooklyn was waiting at the park. Lola had instructed them all to meet there at midday. She sighed and glanced around to see Tai walking towards her.

"Hey." he said cheerfully, she smiled back at him.

"Hi Tai." she greeted as he leant against the park bench with her engaging in conversation as they waited for the other two.

After a while two opposites could be seen getting out of a rather glamorous car.

"Brooklyn! You will not believe how awesome Lola's apartment is!" Jia exclaimed running over and hugging the brunette. Lola followed quietly as the car drove off.

"Shut up Jia." she said, as Jia let go of Brooklyn. "So can you give us any information about this woman?" Lola asked, getting right to the point as she folded her arms staring at Brooklyn. Brooklyn shook her head.

"Not really. Other than her name is Kumiko."

"I thought it would be more alien than that." Jia noted, tilting her head to the side. Brooklyn smiled slightly as Tai pushed away from the park bench.

"No use staying still, let's walk and talk." he said and they all began to walk with him around the park.

"She mentioned the gems and listening to your dreams." Brooklyn explained, causing Lola to let out a groan.

"So she's crazy. Great."

"She doesn't sound crazy Lola. She was right about the gems and about the marks." Brooklyn said showing her wrist as Jia did the same and giggled happily. Tai sighed and glanced around heading to the edge of the park.

"Yeah I found one of those too." he explained, showing off his arm. Lola pursed her lips together and nodded.

"Where is yours Lola?" Jia asked, moving closer to the red head. Lola's eyes widened, and she flicked Jia's forehead.

"None of your business." She snapped, as they left the park to carry on their search.

It was nearing sunset when the group were getting restless.

"Okay. What are we looking for?" Jia asked sitting on the pavement. Lola tapped her foot as Tai and Brooklyn leant against a lamppost.

"Do you not remember anything about where you were?" Tai asked. Brooklyn shook her head and lowered her gaze.

"Sorry guys. I'm new here so I don't really know…" She trailed off as Lola straightened.

"You headed to the docklands from Kumiko right?" she asked. Brooklyn nodded staring at Lola as she flicked her hair over her shoulder. "Which way did you come from?" Lola asked, before making a move, the trio following her.

"Uh…" Brooklyn blushed as Lola shook her head, whilst Jia and Tai each placed a hand on her shoulder and smiled, making her feel a little less useless.

"Brooklyn, you're going to walk the way you arrived at docklands, does that make sense?" she instructed. Brooklyn nodded, and the group picked up their pace as they made their way to the docklands.

Once they had arrived Brooklyn glanced around, the way she had previously come becoming clear and she began to run, the others following with Lola complaining about running in her shoes. They kept going until Brooklyn slowed down and stopped, her eyebrows knitting together in confusion.

"I don't remember anything else." she said softly. Lola nodded and glanced around.

"This is like the edge of Silver Valley." Jia noted. Tai was scanning the area when he spotted Lola hold up a finger.

"That's brand new." she pointed out with the three turning to look in Lola's direction and in the distance was a shimmering building. Jia bounded forward and grabbed Brooklyn's hand.

"Come on!" she beamed and they ran for the building. As they got closer, they spotted a rainbow-coloured sign reading Altair Sweet Shop. The four stopped but it did not look open. Brooklyn reached forward and pushed on the door, it opened, and they walked in greeted by bright lights and a woman standing right in the heart of the shop.

"Finally."

The four stared at the woman, mouths ajar. The woman gestured to a table and walked towards it; the group followed. She stood at the top of the table and the group of friends sat down around it.

"I'm glad to see you found me. I am Kumiko Ito, and I am here to help you." said. The group stared at her in silence, taking her in. She had short light brown hair, with a very upright posture. In her glasses and black turtleneck and white suit trousers she was clearly standing with purpose.

"There isn't much point telling you everything now. But what I can tell you is that there are more of you." she explained. Lola had a puzzled frown.

"And why can't you give us *all* the details?" she demanded. Kumiko looked at her and adjusted her glasses on her nose.

"Because I would have to do it all again when the others get here." she answered. Tai gave a small smirk as Jia giggled. Brooklyn and Lola exchanged glances and Brooklyn turned to Kumiko.

"What can you tell us?" she asked. Kumiko looked at her and sighed.

"There are twelve of you. You all have a mark," she pointed to Brooklyn's wrist. "You all have a gem. You all have a invocation." she stated,

"What sort of invocation?" Brooklyn asked. Kumiko stared at her.

"To help you transform, in dire situations. As you know, there will be creatures out to stop you." she added. Tai sat up straighter.

"The one who walked out of the car? Mala, the bringer of nightmares?" he said causing Jia to shudder.

"Nightmare is right. I can't get her creepy face out of my head." she whined. Kumiko nodded.

"Yes. Now. I suggest you go and start finding the others." she instructed.

"Hold on just a second!" Lola blurted standing up out of her seat. "I have questions! And lots of them too, why were we chosen? Can we give this up if we don't want to be involved?" Lola almost yelled. Tai grabbed her wrist, and she shrugged him off. Kumiko stared at her blankly.

"That's your choice. But no, you can't give up the gem. It belongs to you. If you want to let your friends down." she gestured to the door. "You can go." Kumiko stared Lola down. Tai, Jia and Brooklyn stared at Lola.

"You don't really want to leave?" Jia asked quietly, Lola looked at the ground, Kumiko's gaze too much for her.

"I I just ha-" she trailed off and Tai stood up and placed his hand on Lola's shoulder.

"We'll help you L.A. I promise." he said giving her a smile. Lola looked up at him, seconds ticking by.

"Stop with the L.A…" she murmured, "Okay fine, let's get on with this." she said at length. The trio nodded, smiles lighting up their faces. Kumiko looked satisfied.

"Alright, I will always be here. See you soon." she said as the group headed out of Altair.

Jia stretched her arms above her head before turning to the others.

"Okay first thing Monday morning we start looking for the others!" she declared. Tai nodded in agreement. Jia delved into her pocket.

"Oh my gosh!" she screamed, the trio looked at her as she began pulling everything out of her pockets. Brooklyn stepped forward.

"Are you okay Jia?" she asked as they watched Jia frantically search her pockets. Lola licked her lips, her frustration growing as Jia's look turned to mortification.

"The gem! I lost the gem!" she squealed, this snapped everyone to attention, and they began to panic.

"Did we just get told not to lose them?" Lola asked. Brooklyn gave her a 'not-the-time' look.

"Have you checked every pocket?" Tai suggested, and Jia nodded until her face relaxed, and she took off her boot.

"I put it somewhere safe." she smiled happily. Tai and Brooklyn laughed as Lola rolled her eyes.

"Crisis averted, now I am going home." Lola said staring at Jia for a moment. "Don't lose it." she said as she watched Jia rub her cheek happily against the Amethyst. Tai ruffled Jia's hair and turned to Lola and Brooklyn.

"Alright I'm gonna walk Jia home, see you girls on Monday." he said, giving them a wave as the two headed off. Brooklyn watched them go before turning to Lola.

"I'm glad you're staying Lola." she said softly. Lola's eyes widened in surprise before she scowled and folded her arms.

"Yeah whatever. I'll see you on Monday." huffing before flicking her hair over her shoulder and walking in the opposite direction. Brooklyn watched her go and smiled slightly before she began making her own way home.

Chapter 11 Shadow

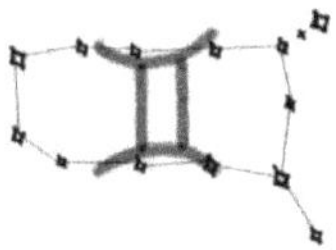

He stared at her, his eyes focused, analysing her, as she walked alone in the streets. He had been sent to retrieve the gems, but once he arrived, he was intrigued by one of the gem holders. In the few days he had been there, he found nothing special about the place, in fact it was dull. He had watched the four gem holders, each one as ridiculous as the other, however she stood out to him. She kept quiet, but he could see she was thinking, analysing her situations. He smirked, knowing now was the time.

Brooklyn walked along the street after another long day of school.

"I wonder what the invocation is..." she murmured to herself. She had her eyes on her phone, messaging Jia when she felt she was being watched. She raised her eyes and looked around her, pulled her jacket closer and gripped her bag tightly. A gust of wind blew around her; hair slapping her in the face. When a boy no older than her jumped down in front of her, her eyes widened in surprise and she took a step back as he reached his hand out taking hers in his, his lips brushing against the back of her hand.

"Now this is going to be fun." the stranger mused. Brooklyn's jaw dropped as he straightened up; his eyes were piercing green.

"Who are you?" she demanded.

"Cato, and I need that." He reached forward to her, her hand immediately went to the gem resting inside her pocket, stepping back again.

"No."

"Come on kitten, don't be like that." he muttered as he reached again, Brooklyn shook her head firmly.

"He's one of them. Like Mala." she thought. Cato reached towards her face and Brooklyn smacked his hand away before running in the opposite direction. Cato blinked, before running after her.

Brooklyn launched herself over the gate and ran through the park, heading down the road towards the docklands. Her heartbeat rapid in her chest, her lungs filling with air as she ran faster.

"This is a dire situation, right? Why can't I transform?" she thought to herself as she took a sharp turn to the left.

"Stop!" He yelled behind her, he was gaining on her, she skidded to a stop as she stared over the edge. Being new to a city was going to be a problem for her. As she stared down, she could see the docklands were further over. She felt a thud and stumbled forward, as arms wrapped around her. She let out a scream as they tumbled down the cliff side.

Cato landed with a thump on top of her, and he stared down at her. Brooklyn groaned and opened her eyes, she let out a gasp and brought her fist up, only for him to catch it.

"Get off of me!" she yelled, he shook his head and she wriggled desperately trying to get away.

"Just give me the gem." he ordered. Making a quick decision Brooklyn stopped wriggling and brought her head up swiftly, head butting him hard in the nose. He let out a shocked yelp and covered his nose, giving Brooklyn enough room to wriggle out from under him, she stumbled back and turned around. A voice whispered in her head;

SAY THE WORDS!

Brooklyn, felt a wave of heat surge through her body, emanating from the mark on her wrist.

"What words?"

YOU KNOW THEM!

Her mouth opened as the words began to flow freely before she even had time to think.

"In the middle of twilight, when stars align, make my powers shine!" Brooklyn's eyes widened in surprise at the words she spoke. The gem in her pocket began to glow a silver hue before the light burst out of the pocket top, a shimmer of silver dust began to swirl around Brooklyn, her eyes shut as she felt something pull her hair up, her body glowed bright as it began to be encased by a diamond looking pattern.

Cato watched on and took a step back, as her clothes began to morph into a silvery skirt, with a white underlay, a silver one shoulder corset and her hair now silver with a feathered steampunk wristband, and silver glittery steampunk heels. The light show faded and Brooklyn gawped at herself, she stared at her hands, a slight shimmer could be seen as she turned her hands around, catching the sunbeams.

She ran her fingers through her tied up hair, and her gem, glowing silver, now floated against her clavicle. Brooklyn snapped out of her trance when Cato cleared his throat.

"That was a mistake." he hissed, eyeing her. Brooklyn shook her head and scowled at him, standing firm.

"No, it was your mistake to attack me first." she stated. Cato sighed, his body began to morph; his pointy elf ears changing into green horns, his body became scaly, and his teeth and nails grew sharper. Brooklyn gasped in shock and found herself stepping back once more.

"Sorry." His voice gruff before he let out a roar. Brooklyn covered her ears and the ground below her began to rumble. Brooklyn stared at him; a green grotesque monster was standing at least seven feet in front of her. She let out a scream as the monster jumped at her, falling to the side and narrowly missing the razor claws.

She flinched and stared down at her knee, covered in grazes. The ground began to rumble again, and Brooklyn looked up to see him running at her, she squealed and scrambled to her feet and began to run. Brooklyn stopped suddenly when a bright blue whip smashed into the ground, causing Cato to stop as well.

Brooklyn and Cato turned their heads to see a stranger clad in leather, the blue hues shimmering in the sunlight. Cato frowned at the newcomer before he jumped up and lunged at him. A fight ensued as Brooklyn slumped to the ground and sat there, her mouth wide, as each flash and clash of whip on claw sounded, she could not move, she could not believe this was happening.

Cato gritted his teeth together, before he turned back to normal and jumped back as the newcomer landed behind Brooklyn. Cato stared at her, a frustrated sigh leaving his lips.

"Next time." he said and he disappeared. Brooklyn was about to speak when she heard her name in the distance.

"Brooklyn!" Jia yelled and ran towards her with Tai and Lola hot on her heels. Brooklyn turned to face them, and her stress and fear melted away as she sighed in relief.

"Jia."

Chapter 12 Partners

"You look amazing!" Jia gushed, jumping around Brooklyn, and inspecting her outfit. Brooklyn blushed as Tai stared at her and Lola sighed rubbing her forehead. Once the trio had arrived, Brooklyn explained to them what had happened, and how close she had been to losing that fight.

"Thanks Jia. And thanks guys for showing up." she said. Lola dismissed her words and turned to the boy behind her.

"Who are you?" she questioned but the boy did not respond, slowly walking forward with his clothing morphing back to his normal clothes, his gem falling into his palm. Jia stopped and straightened.

"It's you!" she squeaked. The boy stood in front of Brooklyn and stared at her, her eyes replied in kind.

"You should be careful, to not transform in the open like that." he said. Brooklyn felt her cheeks redden and she nodded, allowing her body to morph her back to normal, her brown hair fell around her shoulders, and she shuffled uncomfortably.

"Uh, Brooklyn." Tai began pointing at her coat pocket so she looked down to see a burning hole as the gem fell out and onto the ground. Brooklyn gasped and bent down, picking it up and cradling it in her palm as Jia turned to the boy.

"You're the boy from the other day." Jia exclaimed, walking forward and standing in front of him. "Xander. I thought you brought that monster that attacked me." She continued staring up at him wide eyed. "I guess you're one of us." she added, Xander gave a small nod as Jia looked around him. "So where's your mark?" she asked. Xander's eyes flicked to Tai and Lola.

"Is she always like this?" he asked and they both nodded in response. Sighing he turned back to Jia as she was lifting his arms.

"It's on my leg." he answered. Jia stopped and dropped his arm before holding up her leg allowing her trouser leg to fall revealing her mark.

"Same!" she said excitedly. Brooklyn stared at Jia's mark and frowned.

"Why are they the same?" Tai asked. Xander folded his arms as Lola walked closer towards the group.

"We can ask Kumiko. I'm sure she'd have an answer." she muttered. Tai turned to Xander and asked

"Have you found anyone else?"

"I've only found you." he replied. The group exchanged glances before they decided to make their way to see Kumiko.

Once the group had arrived, they noticed a line outside Altair Sweet Shop. Jia frowned and the group began to move closer.

"What's going on here?" Brooklyn asked a group of girls.

"Oh, it's a new sweet shop! And it sells sweets!" one exclaimed, another nodded in agreement. Jia leant over to Brooklyn.

"I figured it would sell sweets." she whispered, causing a gentle smile to spread on Brooklyn's lips.

"Out of this world sweets!" another said excitedly.

"My friend said a really cute guy works there!" she giggled. Brooklyn raised an eyebrow as Lola huffed and walked past the line and straight in, Tai turned to the waiting girls who protested loudly and he smiled at them brightly and began to explain Lola's behaviour as Jia gestured to Xander and Brooklyn to follow. Brooklyn stared at Tai as the girls gushed over him and hung on to every word before she followed Jia.

As she entered, she noticed the place was full, and felt no surprise at seeing an attractive male behind the till and taking orders. Lola was currently at the till, asking for Kumiko. The woman in question walked out from the kitchen a blank expression on her face.

"Perfect, you're here." she said and walked back in. Brooklyn frowned and they followed her in as the boy waved at them, before turning back to the customer Lola had so rudely interrupted.

"I suppose congratulations are in order. You found another member." Kumiko droned. Brooklyn nodded and explained.

"Xander is really strong, he stopped that guy from taking my gem."

Kumiko nodded, keeping her expression blank. Jia sat down as Lola leant against the kitchen table.

"Well, they're making their moves. You must all stay on high alert. I cannot express how important it is to find your whole team." she said. Tai walked in, and they all looked at him.

"What did I miss?" he asked,

"Nothing." Brooklyn said shortly, causing Tai to raise his eyebrow and Brooklyn silently cursed herself before Lola spoke up.

"How many are there of us?" she asked,

"You already asked that."

Lola and Brooklyn straightened in annoyance. As usual Kumiko wasn't being helpful.

"How do we find them?" Brooklyn asked. Kumiko turned away from them and folded her arms.

"That I cannot tell you. They could be just about anyone. Anyone worthy, anyone with hope, love. Emotions that were heightened when the gems arrived. That is all I can give you." She turned back to face them. Brooklyn, Jia, Tai, Lola and Xander exchanged looks as Kumiko gestured to the door. Jia stepped forward, "Wait, why are Xander's and my mark the same?" she asked. Kumiko turned to them, her eyebrow raising slightly.

"So quickly?" She thought to herself before speaking out loud, "Every Zodiac will have a partner to work with, we have always worked in two. But that is a story for another day. I suggest you get started. Perhaps even get to know each other." she said. The group felt a strange energy surround them and suddenly they were outside the sweet store. The group looked around, and Jia wobbled grabbing Brooklyn to steady herself.

"She's quite powerful." Xander commented adjusting his glasses. Lola sighed and began walking in the opposite direction. The others followed quietly behind her.

They had not walked for very long when Tai piped up.

"Zodiac sounds so..." Tai trailed off and Brooklyn tilted her head toward him, quizzically.

"Unbelievable?" Lola offered, "Zodiacs aren't real." she added examining her nails as Xander cleared his throat, taking off his glasses.

"I think you need to separate fact from fiction. I would be inclined to side with you Lola, but the reality is, Brooklyn and I did transform." he stated. Lola sighed and nodded.

"Now we just gotta find the others." Tai confirmed. Brooklyn sighed.

"How do we find them though?" she asked. Everyone looked thoughtful for a moment. Xander folded his arms over his chest.

"We could look into the security cameras around the docklands and see if anyone else was there that night, at least with Zodiac it does narrow it down to twelve people." he suggested. Tai agreed.

"That's a great idea! L.A. do you think you'll be able to pull some footage?" Lola frowned at them.

"It'll take a few days, I don't have access to security, and I don't know how to find the right footage." She explained, clearly not convinced she make the idea work. Xander cleared his throat.

"I can help you." he suggested. Lola's face brightened at the offer.

"I guess that's settled then. Whilst you two are looking at security footage, we can see if anyone is experiencing anything out of the ordinary." Brooklyn suggested

"You're making it sound like it's a disease." Tai mused as Jia giggled. Brooklyn rolled her eyes as Lola scoffed.

"Might as well be… but she's right it would be good to look around the school to see if anyone is there. Now if you'll excuse me, I have to be at home, to cook dinner." she said beginning to walk away as she flicked her hair over her shoulder. Xander nodded.

"I have to go as well." he said. Tai began walking with Xander.

"Yeah, I bailed on dinner for this." he chuckled. Jia held up her hands and grabbed Lola and Xander.

"WAIT!" she yelled even though everyone had stopped. Lola raised an eyebrow and stared down at her hand.

"Let go Jia. Thank you." she insisted, Jia let go, blushed a little and began rummaging in her bag.

"I uh, have something for everyone." she explained. "I was thinking, that carrying the gems in our pockets is a definite easy way to lose them."

"Why? Because you almost lost yours?" Lola teased. Tai shook his head and Jia nodded as she continued rummaging in her bag. She pulled out several bracelets and necklaces, handed one to each of them and held hers up.

"So, I made these, they all have a resemblance to each of our gems and clearly what our zodiac is." She held up her gem and placed it in the hole where it clicked into place and sparkled, her fingers traced over the pattern. Jia had made them with Zodiacs in mind.

"How do you do that?" Tai asked softly, Jia wasn't paying him attention as she hopped from foot to foot clearly excited. Lola stared at hers, it was green with a shimmering sparkle across it, and stars in the shape of Virgo. A small charm of a kitten on it, Lola traced her finger over it.

"Why is there a cat? And a Virgo sign?" She asked, confused, Brooklyn held hers up in silver with a small horse.

"I dunno, I just felt like this was you." Jia said nonchalantly. Accepting the gift Xander strapped his bracelet around his wrist as the girls secured necklaces around their necks.

"Thank you Jia, now I must be off." Xander bid them all goodbye, and Tai did the same and the two boys left.

"See you later." Lola said as she left, her green gem sparkling in the light illuminating her pale skin as she turned, leaving Jia and Brooklyn to walk themselves home.

Chapter 13 Unreal

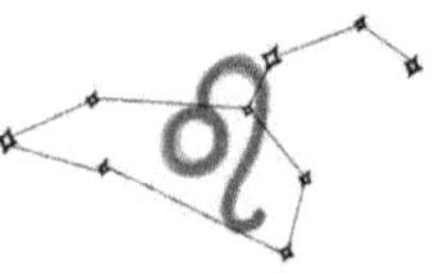

The next day arrived and during a free period Brooklyn and Jia were running around the school invading personal spaces until Brooklyn came to a boy with blonde shaggy hair and his group of friends.

"Hey there, do you have a mark?" Brooklyn asked, looking around. The boys gave her a weird look until the blonde chuckled.

"You okay there?" he asked. Brooklyn looked sheepish and clasped her hands behind her back.

"Hi, sorry, I'm just looking for someone who likes to draw. Body art." She stammered. The other boys laughed, and the blonde raised his eyebrow before turning to his friends.

"I got this you guys, see you in class." he said, giving them a smile. As a collective the boys turned and walked on as he moved to face Brooklyn.

"So, you're the new girl Brooklyn. I'm Allister, I'm in the other class." he announced, to which Brooklyn nodded

"Well, I really need to go. Find, body art..." She took a step back and Allister pulled down his collar and sat at the base of his neck was a mark.

"You mean like this?" He said. Squinting her eyes as if to gain more focus Brooklyn reached for his neck and traced her finger along it. She smiled and glanced up at Allister.

"I've found you!" she said in relief. Allister smirked, as she retracted her fingers, colouring.

"I guess you did." he mused. Brooklyn pursed her lips together and fiddled with her fingers as she glanced around the quiet corridor.

"Listen Allister, we need to talk about that mark and what it can do." she explained in a lowered tone. Allister nodded and quickly grabbed her hand before dragging her into a nearby closet. Brooklyn's eyes widened as he pushed her to the wall gently and closed the door behind him and switched on the light.

"Talk missy." he ordered, and Brooklyn blinked a few times. This was a small space and she noticed every detail about him. His eyes were enchanting, aqua and open, his nose had cute freckles and a smirk that could make anyone swoon.

"Oh right... we've been chosen, to stop these creatures." She waved her hands around and pulled a face, making herself look scary. Allister held back a laugh and nodded as she continued on "and in doing so we've got these gems." Brooklyn pointed to her necklace and Allister nodded, taking it all in.

"Each of us have something to do with the Zodiac except Kumiko, she's kind of like our guide, but she's pretty awful at it, that's all we really know and that you're the sixth member." She explained, her eyes finally meeting his.

"Right, well that sounds…"

"Bizarre?" Brooklyn interrupted. Allister grinned and leaned his hand next to her head.

"I was gonna say interesting but bizarre will do." he said. Brooklyn was about to respond when the door opened and the two of them looked towards the door. Tai frowned as he stared at Allister.

"Long time no see Tai." Allister mused, pulling his arm down and shoving his hands in his pockets. Tai glanced at Brooklyn and back at Allister, before pinching the bridge of his nose.

"Don't tell me…" He trailed off, and Allister moved away from Brooklyn and stood close to Tai.

"Guess I'm one of you." he smirked. Tai let out a defeated sigh and gestured to Brooklyn.

"Come on, class has started." he said ignoring Allister. Brooklyn nodded and walked to Tai who placed his hand on her back and led her down the corridor.

"When are we meeting?" Allister asked, Brooklyn felt Tai's fingers push against her lightly and she glanced back at Allister.

"Tonight, at the new café. Altair." she confirmed and Allister nodded.

"See you there Brooklyn!" he called as Tai rolled his eyes and pushed Brooklyn towards their class.

"What was that about?" she asked. Tai shrugged his shoulders causing Brooklyn to frown. "Alrighty don't tell me." she huffed, Tai rolled his eyes as he opened the door and they walked through. A few girls spotted Tai and shuffled, gesturing for him to sit next to them, however Tai made a beeline for the back of the room pulling a blushing Brooklyn with him, as she watched the girls glare daggers at her.

"Allister and I… we go way back to when we were kids." he muttered as he let go of Brooklyn's hand and sat down with a sigh. Brooklyn sat down next to him and nodded. "But we drifted, different groups and all." He added glancing around the classroom.

"Fun." Brooklyn muttered as she pulled out her history book from her bag. Tai looked at her, puzzled.

"That's it?" he asked. Brooklyn nodded.

"I'm not going to pry… much." she mused giving him a small smile. Tai raised an eyebrow slightly and returned the smile. "Just sounds like it sucks." she added as the teacher walked in, turned her head to the front of the class and rested her chin in her palm as Tai stared at her for a moment longer before turning to his history book.

At the end of the day Tai and Brooklyn met up with each other and walked with pointless chatter to join the others.

"What took you so long?" Lola snapped, when Brooklyn and Tai walked up to the group.

"Sorry." Brooklyn said as Tai gave Lola a smile.

"What did we miss?" He said as Xander gestured for the group to start walking. Tai caught up with him, walking side by side. Jai smiled and bounded on ahead with Lola following with her arms folded but before she could follow, Brooklyn froze.

"Hey gorgeous."

An arm wrapped around Brooklyn's neck and her eyes slowly widened as her head turned to the side to see the guy from yesterday.

"Guys…" she murmured, the group turning around. Tai gritted his teeth together as Lola, Jia and Xander took a step forward.

"It's you…" Brooklyn muttered shakily as he tilted his head slightly and kept his grip on her.

"Cato." he answered, as the group took another step forward. Cato glanced at them and smirked.

"No, no. One wrong move and she's toast. Though, I don't really want to hurt her." Cato mused lifting his finger slightly and running the tip gently across her chin. Brooklyn pursed her lips together and averted her gaze from Cato's.

"What do you want?" Tai yelled. Cato's eyes flickered to Tai and he pressed his chin against Brooklyn's head.

"It's simple really. Mistress wants us to get them, gems. This is pretty." His finger brushed the necklace Brooklyn was wearing, "destroy the world, usual bad guy stuff, and I need you to stay out of the way. Do we have a deal?" he continued.

"Not a chance!" Jia shouted; Cato shook his head.

"Sorry but… It's not your call." He raised his finger to the sky, and everyone looked up to see a giant purple cloud spread across the central area of Silver Valley. Lightning flashed and a loud screech caused the group to cover their ears as a colossal flying creature with talons the size of jeeps, emerged from the purple cloud. Its wings stretching wide like vast, leathery sails, each beat sending ripples through the air. The creature's scales shimmered with an iridescent sheen, reflecting hues of midnight blue. Brooklyn stared up at it, her jaw dropping.

"Stay out of my way kitten and you won't get hurt." Cato whispered. He disappeared and Brooklyn stumbled forward. Tai ran forward putting his hands on her shoulder looking at her with worry.

"I'm fine." She said, noticing his look and he nodded slowly.

"What do we do?" Lola said, placing a hand on her hip.

"We stop him." Tai said firmly. Xander nodded and pushed Jia forward and they headed off towards the creature.

The five of them ran as fast as they could as people ran screaming past them. Xander grabbed Jia's arm, steadying her as someone barged past her.

"Idiots." he muttered under his breath, as Jia blushed.

"Thanks." she muttered. Xander nodded as Brooklyn, Tai and Lola stared up at the creature that was currently using its wings to smash windows on the buildings.

"Okay Brooklyn, how did you and Xander change?" Lola asked, Brooklyn stared at her and it was the first time she'd seen Lola look scared. Xander and Brooklyn exchanged looks and Brooklyn placed her finger on the gem attached to her necklace that Jia gave her, as Xander held up his wrist with the gem attached to the wristband Jia gave him.

"In the middle of twilight, when stars align, make our powers shine!" The two said together, and the gems glowed brightly. A light exploded from each gem, and circled Xander and Brooklyn. In a colourful light display of silvers and blues, Brooklyn closed her eyes and felt the swirling diamonds pull her hair into the high ponytail, as Xander's shoes began to grow in length and turn blue. Both felt an energy run through their bodies, they stared at one another before turning to the others.

Tai, Jia and Lola stared in awe as the two finished glowing. Tai nodded and lifted his wrist.

"These were a great idea Jia." he said, Jia blushed and placed her finger on her gem as Lola did the same.

"In the middle of twilight, when stars align, make our powers shine!" The three echoed the two and their gems burst into life, glowing brightly, and engulfing them in a mixture of glitter and lights. Once the light show had stopped, they all stared at each other, Tai was wearing a similar outfit to Xander, however instead of a long-sleeved jacket, Tai had a brown vest, which was detailed with squared swirls going up along the seams of the vest. Jia had a corset, with a puffy violet skirt. Brooklyn smiled at them until a stamp of a foot and a loud whine caused them to look at Lola.

"Why am I green?" Lola wailed in disgust, as she examined her outfit, she had on a long slit skirt, and her hair had been pulled up into a French plait, her beautiful long red hair had turned an emerald green. Tai chuckled and pushed her along.

"We can discuss our outfits later, come on." he said and ran ahead, Lola rolled her eyes and stomped her way after him.

Chapter 14 Fight

The five had made it to below the creature. It began screeching and swooping, aiming for running pedestrians. Lola gulped and turned to Xander, "Now what?" she asked. Xander stared up at the creature as Jia helped a woman up and pulled her away from the falling debris from the buildings.

"We fight it." Xander said firmly, Tai raised an eyebrow.

"How?" he said as he watched Xander hold out his arm and a blue glow warped around his hand. A whip appeared. He lashed it forward and it snapped against the creature which screeched and turned to the group.

"Well, you got its attention." Tai said, Xander nodded as it began charging at the group. They all let out a scream and dove to the side as the talons slid through the ground. They all dodged out of the way and turned to stare up at the creature.

"What do we do?" Jia asked, hiding slightly behind Tai. Lola glanced around, watching the creature that kept diving to the ground. Her brow furrowed as an idea came to her. She took a couple of steps back getting ready for it to dive again and fly into her pathway.

"Lola!" Brooklyn yelled. Lola stared at her, "what are you doing?"

"I have a plan, duh!" She snapped back. Tai, Xander and Jia stared at her as Brooklyn began to move towards her. The creature began its descent and Lola ran forward.

"Brooklyn!" Lola screamed as she bent slightly and swung her arms back before she back-flipped onto the creature as it skirted the ground before flying back up, she reached her hand out and Brooklyn nodded. The creature sped past once more and Brooklyn jumped up grabbing Lola's hand. The two stood up on the back of the creature, their hair whipping their faces as the creature went higher and faster.

"Okay! We're up here, now what?" Brooklyn yelled as Lola stared at the ground below her.

"Well don't fall off!" she shouted back. Brooklyn deadpanned.

"Obviously!"

"How did Xander get that whip?" Lola asked.

"I'll ask him if we survive this!" Brooklyn yelled back, Lola snorted and stared around her, looking for an answer. Brooklyn inhaled deeply, the air was getting harder to breathe, they weren't invincible, there were limits. She blocked out every thought, until she found something locked away in the back of her mind. She gripped Lola's hand and Lola's eyes widened as a chain locking away her powers broke.

"Now Lola!" Brooklyn called. Lola nodded and flicked her hair over her shoulder as her fingertips began to glow green and a long wooden pole topped with a flat metal blade tapering to a point began to manifest in her hand. A short length of green fabric wrapped its self around the base of the blade completing the polearm.

A silver streak began to glow, winding its way down Brooklyn's arm before a long ribbon appeared in her hand. The ribbon moved on its own and wrapped itself around the creature's wings and trapped them together on the creature. Lola jumped off the creature as it began to fall. Lola yelled. She threw the glowing polearm, and it sliced through the creature.

The creature began to glow and burst into green and silver glitter and disappeared. Lola and Brooklyn cried out as they fell, shutting their eyes tightly in fear as the ground grew closer with every passing second. Xander whipped his whip forward and it wrapped around Lola's waist and he pulled her towards him as Tai and Jia ran forward holding up their arms.

Lola crashed into Xander as Brooklyn landed heavily onto the other two causing them to drop to the ground. Once Brooklyn and Lola were stable and safe on the ground, Lola and Brooklyn exchanged glances, breathing heavily as they changed back to normal, their hair floating gently over their shoulders. Brooklyn took a step forward and a shudder ran up her legs and she dropped to her knees.

"Brook-" Lola fell backwards into Xander's chest, her eyes closing as she fell. Xander placed his hands on her upper arms holding her steady. Tai ran to Brooklyn as she fell sideways and grabbed her, gently cradling her in his arms as her eyes closed just like Lola's.

"Are they okay?" Jia asked, worry in her voice. Tai stared at Brooklyn, completely out cold.

Tai hauled Brooklyn onto his back gently as Xander picked Lola up, Jia stood with a wary expression on her face.

"I think we need to see Kumiko. They should not have collapsed like this." He said softly, as they began to hurry towards Altair Sweet Shop.

Cato stared down at the group, as they disappeared around the corner and out of sight and rested his chin on his palm.

"That was fun to watch." he mused to himself, sighing and staring. up at the sky. "Though, it could have gone better." He stood up and stretched his arms above his head. "They aren't very strong right now." He turned to the creatures behind him, swaying and disappearing in and out of the shadows. He smirked, and he jumped off the tower.

"See you soon kitten." And he disappeared.

"Kumiko!" Tai yelled, slamming the door open. The group had made it to the sweet store, and they rushed in as Kumiko glanced up, her expressionless eyes landing upon Lola and Brooklyn. "They collapsed after the battle." He said as he brought them to an empty table and laid Brooklyn down as Xander did the same for Lola. Kumiko got up out of her chair as Jia closed the door behind her. Kumiko pressed her hand against the girls' foreheads and raised their wrists, checking their pulses.

"They'll be fine." she said as she glanced at the necklaces on the girls, a smaller flicker of light coming from them.

"Why did they collapse?" Jia asked and Kumiko looked at her.

"Exhaustion. Nothing fatal." she explained, Tai and Xander sighing in relief. "They aren't used to the power of the gems yet. If you overexert yourselves, you'll be tired. Let them rest for a while. Well done." she said and walked away.

The boys sat down next to each other as Jia sat between the two girls and pulled out her notebook, beginning to draw with silence filling the room as the trio waited quietly for the girls to wake up.

The door opened and Allister walked in, he frowned as he spotted everyone gathered around a sleeping Brooklyn and Lola.

"What did I miss?" he asked, Tai didn't respond as he stared at Brooklyn whilst Xander and Jia turned to him.

"Who are you?" Xander asked as Kumiko walked back in from the kitchen.

"How am I supposed to earn money if I shut down every time you all have a problem?" she sighed before finally spotting Allister.

"Taurus?" she queried. Xander, Tai and Jia glanced up and Allister raised his eyebrow.

"My name's Allister." he said. Kumiko slowly blinked and turned to Tai and the others.

"So, Taurus?" Tai asked suspiciously. Kumiko sighed and sat down on an empty chair.

"Have you all figured out your Zodiacs?" she asked and Jia shook her head.

"It appears to have slipped our minds. Fighting giant birds and all." Xander said sarcastically. Kumiko nodded thoughtfully. Tai sighed.

"You're not going to tell us, are you?" he muttered as Allister walked towards Lola and Brooklyn.

"Oh!" Jia blurted and rummaged in her jacket pocket pulling out a picture. "I started drawing these! Do you think that'll help?" she asked, opening the folded paper and putting it on the table. The three boys came over to Jia and stared at her picture for a while until Xander pointed to one of them.

"That is an emerald with Virgo." He said pointing to a swirly image that blended several shades of green with the symbol of Virgo. Tai focused on that, and Jia nodded, as Allister looked at her.

"Are you a witch?" he asked. Jia frowned at him, and he shrugged his shoulders in response.

"Don't be rude." she huffed, "I'm not a witch... besides there's nothing wrong with being a witch." she murmured; Tai ruffled her hair.

"She's intuitive. Xander you're right and look at this one, it's the Capricorn sign, right? It's silvery just like Brooklyn's outfit was." he said. Xander nodded in agreement.

"Just like the design on our bracelets and their necklaces you made us." Xander said looking at Jia. Kumiko watched them all quietly from the sideline, a flicker of a smile washed over her features before she went back to her blank stare.

"They're learning... but how will it end your majesty?" she thought to herself as she stared at the children in front of her. "They're so much younger than them." She closed her eyes and stayed silent as the group figured out their destinies.

Chapter 15 Teammate

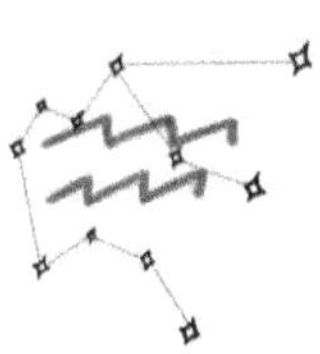

After a few hours Lola and Brooklyn began to stir. Tai was the first to notice and he jumped up and hurried to Brooklyn's side.

"You okay?" he asked as Brooklyn slowly sat up and glanced around.

"What happened?" She asked, her eyes landed on Lola who was lying next to her, "Lola!" She exclaimed. Lola's eyes twitched, opened and glanced up at Brooklyn.

"I'm fine." She muttered and, taking Allister's hand to help her, sat up as the others had gathered around. "What did we miss?"

"Not much," Jia answered. Xander adjusted his glasses and folded his arms.

"But we may have found some answers."

The two girls nodded and Allister propped his arms behind his head and smiled.

"We found out that Jia is a witch. Xander had been looking at the footage you pulled up and found a few people that were at the docklands the same time we all were." he explained. Brooklyn glanced at him as Tai rolled his eyes.

"What were you doing there?" she asked. Allister tapped his nose and Lola scoffed and swung her legs delicately off the table.

"I don't know about you. But I have other responsibilities to get on with. Shall we call it a day?" she said. Tai glanced at the clock on the wall and gave a slight nod. Jia pouted,

"But it was just getting good." she whined; Brooklyn smiled slightly as Lola rolled her eyes.

"Does the princess have to tend to the castle?" Allister teased. Lola scoffed and stood up as Xander cleared his throat.

"I have some other matters to attend to." he stated. Brooklyn stood up and Jia bounded over linking arms with her.

"Alright, I guess see you all tomorrow?" she asked. Tai, Xander, Jia and Allister nodded and they all looked at Lola who was studying her nails until she felt everyone's eyes on her. She frowned before sighing in defeat.

"Fine, I will see you all tomorrow." And with that the group headed outside, Xander going one way, Allister, Lola and Jia going the other, leaving Tai and Brooklyn on the doorstep of Altair Sweet Shop.

"Wanna walk home?" Tai asked and Brooklyn glanced up at him, a blush forming on her cheeks as she nodded. He gestured to the right and Brooklyn stepped in front and began walking with Tai following next to her.

"So that was intense." Tai mused. Brooklyn looked up at him and noticed he had a small frown on his face, not matching his tone.

"Yeah, but we sorted it." she said. Tai nodded, and his eyes flickered to her before running his hand through his hair absently.

"We have got a lot to do, and I think we need to train and get your stamina up." he said. Brooklyn raised her eyebrow.

"No thanks." she stated bluntly. Tai snapped out of his thoughts and chuckled.

"That was a definitive no." he chuckled; Brooklyn nodded.

"You do *not* want to train Me." she said, Tai laughing as they stopped at a crossing.

"It couldn't hurt to shape up." Nudging her shoulder, "you passed out."

"So did Lola." Brooklyn scoffed; Tai nodded.

"Yeah but L.A is hard to convince to do anything." he explained. Brooklyn nodded and the two crossed the road.

"Why do you call her L.A? She doesn't seem to like it." Brooklyn asked. Tai shrugged his shoulders.

"Her name is Lola Anderson and she moved from Lagoona Aqronte. It just works." He smiled and Brooklyn hummed softly. "Where are you from?" he asked suddenly. Brooklyn glanced up at him.

"Mistvorne. I know like, a whole world away." she answered. Tai nodded thoughtfully. "What about you?" she asked awkwardly.

"Lived here all my life." He ran his hand through his hair, as they crossed the street.

The two had made it to Brooklyn's house and they walked up the path quietly. Brooklyn knocked on the door and Tai tilted his head to the side. She held up a finger.

"Just wait."

"Brooke why did you forget your keys!" The two of them heard a shrill shout come from the other side of the door and then it flew open.

"Well, hey Kayleigh." Tai said bending down. Kayleigh's eyes lit up and she jumped into Tai's arms.

"You're back!" she exclaimed laughing happily. Tai chuckled and let go of her. "Are you staying?" she asked. Tai shook his head and Brooklyn rolled her eyes at her sister who pouted.

"Sorry, but I should be getting home." He straightened up and turned to Brooklyn, he reached his hand out and ruffled her hair giving her a smile.

"See you later." he said and walked past her. Brooklyn watched him go and smiled slightly. Kayleigh stared at her sister and clasped her hands behind her back.

"This place isn't so bad." she teased and ran back inside as Brooklyn sighed and headed inside the house closing the door behind her.

The next day, Jia, Lola, Brooklyn and Xander had gathered at Silver Valley's library as Allister and Tai had after school activities. Meanwhile Lola was staring incredulously at the monitor screen.

"From what I could gather, she is at your school." Xander explained, "I believe she is in the year above you. Clean record, two siblings and a father, tends to keep to herself. Do either of you know her?" He directed his question at Lola and Jia. Jia squinted at the screen, and Lola nodded her head furiously.

"I just want to know how you do that?" Jia asked, Xander completely ignoring her.

"No way!" Lola gasped in awe. Brooklyn stared at her, as Jia glanced at the screen again then to Lola.

"I don't get it?" Jia asked.

"There is no way, Harper Collins is… like us!" Lola hissed, staring at the purple haired beauty, her cheeks reddening slightly. The image staring back at her was of a frowning girl with long, purple hair that reached the middle of her back, complemented by a side fringe. Her striking jade green eyes were framed by long, luscious eyelashes coated in mascara.

"There has to be a mistake." She said looking up at Xander, who shook his head in response.

"My mathematical conclusions are never wrong." he said. Lola chewed on her lip. "However, my concoctions are not always as successful." Xander held up a drink and put the straw in Brooklyn's mouth, she gulped the drink down and began spluttering. "Too salty?" he asked blank faced. Brooklyn squealed and hopped up and down causing Jia to laugh.

"Too everything!" She gagged. Xander sighed and adjusted his glasses with one hand and offered the drink to Lola who wrinkled her nose up in disgust.

"Alright, we'll find Harper." she said softly. Jia tilted her head to the side as Brooklyn began pushing her towards the door.

"Did we say something wrong?" Jia asked,

"No idea." Brooklyn answered as they followed Lola out of the library.

"See you soon Harper. Thanks for your help."

Harper nodded and began walking away from the office. She rummaged through her bag and grabbed her headphones and placed them over her hat and ears, closed her eyes slowly and opened them again focusing on the road ahead.

Please. We need you, please, the others are waiting.

"How do you know that?"

Find the others. It is the only way.

"How?"

The light faded and everything went dark, she shook her head recalling her recurring dream. She sighed and pulled her collar up as she walked down the street. She crossed the road and kept going until she came to a stop by her apartment building. She pulled out her keys and walked in, slipped off her jacket and pulled her headphones, hat and shoes off, as she walked through into the kitchen, a heavy sigh left her lips.

"Klara, it was your turn to do the washing up." she muttered, before heading to the kitchen to clean. The hot water trickled down her fingers as she placed the next plate on the draining board, stared at her reflection and her hand brushed the side of her neck, the mark shimmering slightly. She heard the door slam open behind her and she covered her neck back up.

"Going out! Be back later, dad's coming home tonight!" A flash of blonde sped past Harper, and Harper nodded as the front door closed.

Please. We need you.

She stopped washing and glanced around, the voice suddenly appearing in her thoughts. She quickly pulled her hands out of the water and hurried to the door. She grabbed her leather jacket and left the house. Harper glanced left and right.

"How am I supposed to find them?" She thought to herself, feeling a pull towards the outskirts of Silver Valley.

"How are we supposed to find Harper?" Jia asked, Lola shrugged her shoulders as they walked down a street.

"Do you not know?" Brooklyn asked, Lola shook her head.

"She keeps to herself a lot. But she's well known in the Valley." Lola explained. Jia pointed forward.

"Isn't that her?" The two girls followed Jia's finger and spotted a purple haired girl walking quickly in front of them.

"Harper!" Lola shouted and grabbed Brooklyn's arm. "Come on!" she said quickly, and the three girls began to run after Harper.

"Harper stop!" Lola called, the purple haired girl's head lifted and she turned around to see the three girls running at her. She raised an eyebrow, and the trio came to a staggered stop.

"Hi?" Harper said slowly. Lola felt her cheeks redden and she shoved Brooklyn forward.

"Uh. Hi, you don't actually know me but uh… I'm Brooklyn, this is Lola and Jia." Brooklyn said gesturing to the two behind her. "We were wondering if you, have a… mark? Like this one?" She held up her wrist and showed it to Harper, the taller girl frowning and about to speak when a voice cackled.

"I thought I wouldn't find you again."

Brooklyn, Jia and Lola gasped, and Harper looked up at the top of the streetlamp, a woman with blood red hair was sat on top of it grinning.

"Oh, I haven't met you. Maybe I can have a little fun with you too. Once I get what I want from them." She pointed a finger at the trio and Harper stepped in front, her protective instincts taking control.

"Back off." Harper said with a slight growl to her voice. Mala pouted,

"That's not very nice."

"Go away." Harper's eyes narrowed as Lola, Brooklyn and Jia watched Harper.

"No." She jumped down and yanked the light from the ground with little effort and launched it at the girls. Harper shoved Lola and the others out of the way, the four hitting the ground hard. Mala tilted her head to the side and huffed. Harper stood back up, Mala smiled at her and took a step forward.

"You're feisty. I like that." Mala said grinning. Harper pulled off her dirty jacket and retrieved a gem from her pocket and Lola, Jia and Brooklyn stared up at the older girl. Mala's hand began to spark red and slamming her hand through the wall, it cracked and shattered quickly, causing the ground to rumble.

Mala brought her other hand up and pulled back the skin around her lips barring sharp and pointy teeth. Her body began to morph, a tail whipped round and stretched towards Harper,

"Harper!" Lola yelled. Brooklyn grabbed Lola's waist keeping her in place, as Harper stayed still, Mala grinned and folded her arms over her chest.

"I *really* like you." She howled in delight and raced forward as Harper stepped back, bringing her arm up and blocking Mala, again and again until Harper was against the wall. A familiar voice whispered in her head;

Remember what I told you!

Harper, felt a wave of heat surge through her body, emanating from the mark on her neck.

Her mouth opened, the memories of her recent dreams flooding her mind.

"In the middle of twilight, when stars align, make my powers shine!" Harper yelled; Mala stopped in front of Harper as the light engulfed them both. Bright pinks and roses filled the room and once the light faded Harper was standing with a side plait and her hair all in pink, with a pair of shorts and corset like the others, Jia threw a necklace over to her.

"Here!" she yelled. Harper caught the necklace and secured it around her neck quickly and snapped the rose quartz gem in place, narrowly missing Mala's tail.

"You know… I thought you'd be more blood red." Mala scoffed; Harper darted forward knocking the distracted Mala to the ground.

"We have to help." Brooklyn suddenly piped up. Lola and Jia stared at her and nodded. The three girls stood up.

"In the middle of twilight, when stars align, make my powers shine!"

Mala glared at the four that now stood before her as they completed their transformations.

"Fine. Next time. I'll just wait until one of you is all alone and then I'll really have my fun" she hissed out and disappeared. The four girls turned back into their normal clothes and Jia jumped up and down.

"That was super!" she breathed, Harper turned to Lola and Brooklyn.

"You're like me too?" Harper asked, directing her questions at Brooklyn.

"Yeah. There's three more like us, and a couple more that we haven't found yet." She explained. Harper nodded and gestured away from the building.

"Come on, we're too exposed out here." She began walking towards the mall and Lola, Brooklyn and Jia followed.

"Who was that?" Harper asked as Brooklyn jogged next to Harper.

"Oh, her name's Mala, she's after those." She pointed to the gem.

"I see."

"Uh… Harper I'm sorry you're caught up in this." Lola mumbled. Harper glanced at her and gave a small shrug of her shoulder.

"Have you had dreams too?"

Jia bounded forward.

"Yes! And like, I keep seeing these monsters and I'll draw them and then they're real! It's so cool! And then there was your gem with pink colours and silver for Brooke!" She continued and Lola rolled her eyes as Harper, although looking bored, was listening intently to Jia.

"Lola! Jia!" A voice called from afar.

"Brooke!" another yelled. Jia began waving frantically.

"Hey we found another member!" she yelled. Lola nudged Jia harshly.

"Stop saying this out loud, Jia. People will think we're weird." Lola mumbled, Brooklyn watched as Allister, and Tai were running towards them with Xander on their heels, walking slowly. Tai came to a stop in front of Brooke and placed his hands on her shoulders giving her a once over.

"You all okay?" he asked. Brooklyn nodded. Allister smiled at them and shoved his hands in his pockets.

"Shame we weren't here to help out."

"You must be Harper." Xander said adjusting his glasses as he came to a stop in front of the group. Harper nodded as she folded her arms.

Chapter 16 Question

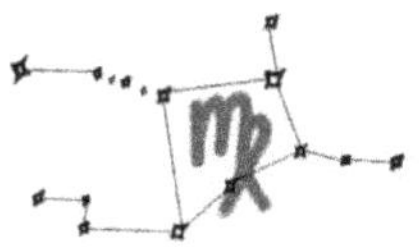

A few days had passed since Harper had joined the team. After being caught up, Harper had agreed to help the others and now Harper let out an annoyed sigh before breathing in deeply.

"If you are going to sit around, you could help by cleaning the tables." she muttered. As soon as Harper had joined, Kumiko had roped her into helping at the sweet shop as she had gone out for 'business' and now she, Brooklyn and Lola were the only three doing any work.

"So Xander, found anyone else?" Allister asked, ignoring Harper as she continued to sweep Altair Sweet Shop.

"Not right now." Xander said staring at the screen, Tai next to him. Jia sat drawing in her notebook as Brooklyn was behind the till serving a customer.

"How did we get roped into this?" Lola asked, sealing the lid on the cup of sweets and turning to give it to the waiting customer. "Would you guys help! Harper already asked you once!" she snapped. Tai, Jia and Allister looked up and Allister stood up yawning.

"No can do, I have to go to practice." he said. Lola's eyebrows narrowed. Jia stared at the clock.

"Oh! I have to help in the kitchen." she added standing up. Lola's eye twitched as she turned her attention to Tai who had a sheepish grin on his face.

"I've got coaching to do."

"You all are useless!" Lola said throwing her hands up in the air and storming into the kitchen. Harper glanced up from the floor.

"Xander any news?" she said, as he sighed and closed the laptop.

"Unfortunately, not." He took his glasses off and rubbed the bridge of his nose. "One image is too blurred."

"Then that's our cue to leave." Allister said with Tai, Jia and Allister edging closer to the door.

"See you." Brooklyn said, as she stacked the final empty shelf with sugary liquorish as Lola came back out.

"Useless." she mumbled and sat back down on a chair as the trio left, laughing and chatting together as they escaped responsibilities, leaving the others to close the shop for the night.

A month had passed, and they were no closer to finding any other members. Cato, and Mala had made it their personal mission to disrupt the Zodiacs' lives. The group collapsed into Altair, after another fight with Mala and an army of small creatures that followed her every command.

"You know, she's horrid." Jia said, sighing as her head hit the table. Brooklyn nodded leaning back on Tai's shoulder as Lola went behind the counter with Harper. Allister stared out the window as Xander went back to his laptop. A routine all too familiar to the others. The door opened and the bell pinged. A group of girls came in chatting and laughing together. Lola chewed on her lip and put on her best smile.

"Hey there, could we get three Charon sweet mixes and one strawberry milkshake and five Altair prism taffeta please?" a girl with long wavy brown hair asked. Lola nodded and Harper turned around to the machine.

"Is that cash or card?" Lola said, as the girl brought up her hand and Lola's eyes widened before she took the card and swiped.

"Did you see Lola." Tai whispered to Brooklyn who leant back further on Tai craning her neck to see Lola.

"Her angry face?" Brooklyn mused. Tai chuckled but shook his head.

"Something about that girl."

"You mean Audrey?" Jia said without lifting her head off the table. Tai and Brooklyn glanced at her.

"Who?"

"How'd you know who it was?" Tai asked. Jia shrugged; her eyes still closed.

"She goes to our school." Jia explained.

"But you didn't even look at her?" Tai said, his comment overlooked as the group of girls left, and Lola hurried over grabbing Brooklyn's arm.

"She has a mark on her!" she hissed, shaking Brooklyn.

"Does she?" Brooklyn breathlessly as Lola shook her harder. Harper walked over and folded her arms, listening to the conversation.

"Yeah. On her wrist." Lola said. Brooklyn pulled back her sleeve, it was shimmering more than usual.

"Did Kumiko ever explain why it's the same?" Jia asked finally looking up from the table.

"Yes Jia." Xander sighed, and she grinned. "I suggest you girls go and see her, Tai and Allister perhaps we should search the perimeter, in case of Cato and Mala?" Xander said standing up. Tai patted Brooklyn's shoulder and she sat up straight as Lola and Jia moved towards her. Harper stared at the group and watched as they began chatting and leaving. Harper rolled her eyes,

"I guess I'm staying here, to work." she sighed; a customer walked in. "How can I help you?"

The next day the three girls met up and headed to the dance and drama building of the school. They watched as the young girl in front of them, with wild black hair and long limbs, Audrey, danced in the studio. Brooklyn, Lola and Jia exchanged looks before walking in and clearing their throats. Audrey spotted them in the corner of her eye and stopped dancing and turned to her dance group.

"Well done today guys!" Audrey said as the group began to leave, she smiled and turned to Brooklyn and Jia giving them both a smile before raising a cold eyebrow at Lola.

"What do you want?" she asked, hostility evident in her voice. Lola frowned.

"What's with the attitude?" she snapped back. Brooklyn and Jia sighed.

"Nothing L.A… just that I've heard everything about you." Audrey said folding her arms over her chest.

"Listen brat. I served you yesterday-" Lola began, but Brooklyn clamped her hand over Lola's mouth and Jia stepped in front of her, smiling at Audrey.

"We were just hoping to have a dance lesson with you and to ask you a few things." she explained. Audrey's eyes lit up.

"Now you're speaking my language! Let's get dancing." she said jumping up and down.

A few hours had passed, and Jia was lying on the floor as Brooklyn was gasping for breath.

"So you guys are saying I have a special ability?" Audrey asked, as Lola nodded.

"If you have one of these," She bent down and picked up Jia's leg allowing her trouser leg to fall and reveal the mark. Audrey walked closer, inspecting the mark as Lola lifted Brooklyn's wrist.

"Oh, yeah it showed up a month ago!" Audrey said, showing off her wrist. Brooklyn, and Jia snapped up and Lola sighed nodding.

"Bingo." She said and Audrey smiled.

"Alright then! What do we gotta do?" she asked. The three girls raised their eyebrows.

"You're not questioning this?"

"Nope."

"Not at all?"

"Nope. Hey Jia! You're meant to be in our year, how's being in higher life treating you?" And the two walked off leaving Lola and Brooklyn confused before they followed the two sixteen-year-olds.

Chapter 17 Date

"Hey mum, dad I'm home." Brooklyn said as she shut the door, she walked in and sat down on the sofa sighing heavily. After introducing Audrey to the others, and having a relatively nice meal together, they had all gone their separate ways for the weekend. Brooklyn glanced around the living room before standing up and moving into the kitchen.

"Kay? Cal? You in?" She called again, as she opened the fridge and shut it again. She aimlessly wandered the house until she found herself back in a quiet living room.

"I guess everyone's still out..." She headed upstairs to her bedroom and flopped onto the bed, shut her eyes and hugged her pillow tightly. How had her life ended up this way? She sighed heavily, her phone buzzed and she opened one eye and grabbed her phone, the light blinding as the phone unlocked.

You busy?

She rolled over onto her back and stared at the message from Tai. She typed back and laid her phone on her chest.

Wanna meet me at the skate park?

She read the message and frowned, where was that? She sat up and stared at the clock and hopped out of bed. Her phone buzzed and she rolled her eyes, a small smile playing on her lips as he laughed at her not knowing where it was. She headed downstairs and opened the front door and headed out.

"Took your time," Tai teased, a playful glint in his eye. Brooklyn rolled her eyes, stepping through the gate with a huff.

"I didn't know where I was going," she replied, prompting a smile from Tai as he gestured toward the ramps.

"Have you skateboarded before?" he inquired, brandishing a skateboard. Brooklyn raised an eyebrow, accepting the board. Their fingers brushing causing them both to blush and glance away. Brooklyn cleared her throat and looked back at him.

"I've roller skated," she answered, placing it on the ground and stepping on, wobbling slightly until Tai reached out, grasping her arm to steady her.

"That'll do. Now, both feet on, give me your hands, and I'll pull you along," he instructed. She complied, and he began to walk backward, guiding her forward.

"Okay! Just don't let go!" she laughed, the thrill of the moment washing over her. Tai chuckled, his eyes sparkling.

"I've got you. Besides, what's the worst that could happen?"

"I fall head over heels?" She humoured causing Tai to laugh.

As they glided along, the world around them blurred into a vibrant canvas of colours and the cooling air brought a gentle rustle of leaves and crickets began their rhythmic symphony. As dusk fell, the sunset's warm hues faded into a deep indigo sky, leaving a tapestry of twinkling stars.

Brooklyn felt a mix of exhilaration and nervousness, but with Tai's steadying presence, she found herself smiling.

"Have you enjoyed being here?" he asked, glancing back at her. Brooklyn lifted her gaze from the ground.

"I suppose; it's not what I was expecting." Brooklyn answered.

"It can be dull here sometimes…" Tai said, thinking about his life in Silver Valley.

"I meant the monsters… the whole superhero thing threw me too." Brooklyn interjected. Tai paused for a moment, then nodded slowly. As the calming silence enveloped them, Tai found himself unable to look away from her. She was so engrossed in her task, her brow slightly furrowed in concentration as she manoeuvred the skateboard with practiced ease. The way her hair caught the light and the subtle smile that played on her lips made his heart race.

"A bit faster?" He said.

"I'll give it a go." Brooklyn nodded, while Tai focused on their feet.

"Yeah, that was… strange. But it makes it a little more exciting," he noted, releasing one of her hands. Brooklyn instinctively raised her hand to maintain her balance. "You know, being a superhero might mean that you have a super power too." He added, Brooklyn raised an eyebrow, intrigued.

"And what would that be?"

"Fearlessness," he replied smoothly, glancing back at her with a playful smirk. "You're already conquering the world of skateboarding, after all."

She rolled her eyes but couldn't suppress her grin. "Am I now?"

"Only because you have the right partner," he said, his voice softening as he looked into her eyes, making her heart skip a beat. There was something about the way he said it that made her feel invincible, as if they could take on anything together.

"Alright, Tai. Let's see how fearless I can be," she declared, her competitive spirit ignited. With a determined nod, she shifted her weight and pushed off a little harder, feeling the rush of air and the thrill of the ride.

"Now that's the spirit!" Tai encouraged, his laughter ringing out like music. He matched her pace, pulling her along effortlessly, their hands intertwined as they enjoyed the liberating rush of the moment, all thanks to the boy who had turned an ordinary night into something extraordinary.

Suddenly, a deafening explosion shattered the air, and they turned to see yellow and amber flames dancing by the docks, dark smoke billowing ominously into the sky. Tai grasped her hand, her eyes widening in alarm.

"Let's go!" he urged. Brooklyn nodded, and together they sprinted toward the flames, leaving the skateboard behind.

"What are you two doing together?" Lola asked, as Tai and Brooklyn met with the others.

"Skateboarding." Tai answered simply, Xander adjusted his glasses and with his free hand pointed to the fire.

"How do we stop it?" Jia asked. Allister shrugged his shoulders.

"Any of us use water?" he laughed. Audrey punched his arm and he flinched.

"Can you focus please." Lola said scolding the two, staring at the fire. Brooklyn glanced around, and flexed her fingers as Jia gripped her necklace.

"Who did this?" Audrey asked, Brooklyn was about to respond.

"Who do you think shortie?"

Audrey's eyes blazed in anger and everyone looked up to see Cato, with his arms folded standing behind a perched Mala who was grinning sadistically.

"I wanted to try out a new move. Turns out there's more flammable things here than I thought." She mused. Lola rolled her eyes as Mala grinned, her eyes scanning everyone until they landed on Harper and she let out a squeal.

"Oh goodie you're here!" She stood up and jumped down, and Cato followed.

"Why are you doing this?" Tai yelled, stepping forward, Mala tilted her head to the side.

"Why do your kind go to war for no reason? Why is there no harmony between any of you?" She asked, "Unlike your kind, we will do whatever it takes to make the mistress happy."

"But blowing up and harming others is wrong!" Jia shouted, Mala raised her finger and wiggled it side to side.

"I don't care." She hummed, a tail whipped around Mala and slashed down in front of the group. Everyone moved to avoid the attack, Brooklyn, Jia, Lola and Tai on one side of the pair whilst Xander, Allister, Audrey and Harper on the other.

The ground erupted into splintering concrete as Cato and Mala sneered at the group, and a darkness began to erupt around the two of them. Brooklyn gulped, as the two let out an ear-splitting roar. Audrey covered her ears as Allister and Lola took a step back and Brooklyn glanced around. Fear. She felt fear.

The wind grew stronger, the air felt constricting to the group and the ground shuddered underneath them. Tai glanced down and Jia gripped his arm tightly, sweat forming on her brow, fear evident in her dark muddy eyes. The two launched forward, running towards the group, Brooklyn stepped forward, earning everyone's attention.

"We've got to move forward. Now." She mustered her courage, and the group hesitated before Allister piped up. Cato and Mala sneered at the group.

"Alright guys, it's time to hero up!" Allister said jumping up and down. Lola frowned at him.

"Can you not be so happy about this." she said, snapping out of her scared state and took a step towards Allister and Audrey as Xander and Tai held up their wrists while Harper, Brooklyn and Jia touched their gems on their necklaces.

"In the middle of twilight, when stars align, make our powers shine."

Lola, Allister, and Audrey glanced at each other before nodding at one another and transforming as well. Cato and Mala watched them quietly,

"You know, we probably should have stopped that." Cato pointed at them, Mala tilted her head at him and shook her head.

"You think?"

"We said we wanted a challenge at full power?" he asked. She growled.

"Yes. You fool." she hissed. As the light from their transformation began to fade the group readied themselves, eyes full of determination which sent Mala spiraling. "Let's take this up a notch!" Mala screeched. Cato rolled his eyes as Mala threw her arms out, oozing shadows dripped from her fingers creating puddles of darkness. Slowly and surely bulging red eyes and slimy creatures clambered over one another out of the puddles. Mala dropped to her knees, squealing excitedly,

"My pretty umbras. Get them." She grinned and the creatures all turned to the group their red eyes seemingly seeing right through the group's souls. Cato and Mala let out a roar and the two morphed as the creatures from the puddle began speeding forwards on all fours.

The group split up, moving away from each other as the creatures charged at them. Mala locked eyes with Harper and Harper took off as Lola was surrounded by small snake like umbras. She held her hands forward and shut her eyes, her fingers began to glow bright green and her polearm appeared. She swung it around her body and it smacked into the creatures, dissolving them with each slice. She lunged forward as one jumped up and she sliced through it, the ooze splattering over her face. She blinked and let out a scream and dropped her polearm, rubbing furiously at her face.

"Lola!"

Lola's eyes widened as Mala was rugby tackled to the side by Harper. Lola rolled and pursed her lips, tears filling her eyes as she turned to the army of creatures running at her; eyes flashing a brighter green she grabbed her polearm and ran at them, rage filling her.

"Harper I'll help you in a minute!" she screamed. She threw her pole arm and it flew through the air and penetrated a creature's eye that burst into ooze. Lola somersaulted over three of them, pulled her polearm back and swung it knocking all the others away.

She let out a breath and used the back of her forearm and rubbed her face, the ooze smearing against her pale skin. She glanced at the others taking in the fight of their lives, eyes falling on Xander, who was holding his own.

Xander's whip hit through an umbra and it spluttered and exploded, he adjusted his glasses and one jumped at him. Xander used his bottle and smacked it in its face, it oozed down his hands; his nose crinkled in disgust.

"Do they have to be so vile?" he muttered, as more surrounded him. "I suppose they are not that intelligent either." he said as he brought his whip up before his head, swinging it around and slashing down on four of them piled together. He sighed and glanced at the group as Jia ran passed screaming as a group of umbras chased her.

Tai and Brooklyn jumped into their path, both protecting Jia. Jia ducked quickly as one flew over the top of her head and she dropped to her knees, her eyes wide in shock. Brooklyn wrapped her ribbon around them as Tai grabbed two bin lids and with all his might symbolled them together causing them to squidge and turn back into ooze.

"Brooklyn look!" Tai said pointing forward. Brooklyn pulled her ribbon back and stared at the group of creatures that were clambering on to one another; growing in size, mangling together. She stepped back until she was shoulder to shoulder with Tai.

"That's gross." She said, Tai nodded in agreement and nudged her with his elbow.

"Well. Shall we?" he mused, she gave a slight smile her cheeks flushing.

"Thought you'd never ask." she said as Tai gave a chuckle. His smile disappeared as he threw his bin lid, the two watched as it smacked into it and slowly slipped down the oozing creature.

"Now you're down a weapon." she said.

"Well it usually comes back in the movies." Tai groaned. Brooklyn shook her head and smiled, taking a step forward as the creature slowly trudged forward.

"This isn't a movie." she teased, he rolled his eyes.

"I would have never guessed. Brooklyn." he said firmly, she glanced at him. "You go low, I'll go high." He ran forward and she panicked.

"I don't understand!" she wailed and Tai smiled as she flicked her wrist and the ribbon floated forward wrapping around the creature. It hovered around the creature, she tugged the ribbon, and it tightened around the creature's legs, its movement stilted. Tai leapt into the air, bin lid first and flew into it, knocking it backwards before repeatedly smacking the creature underneath him until it was just a puddle of ooze. Brooklyn ran forward her ribbon sparkling prettily as it disappeared. Tai stood up wiping his forehead.

"I knew you'd get it." He laughed. Brooklyn placed her hands on her hips and nudged him with her elbow.

"What are they?" Audrey asked as she grabbed a broken fence post and stabbed through one of the creature. The two others hesitated for a moment before diving her. She jumped on top of them, letting out an angry yell and skewered the other two.

Cato stopped his attack on Allister, as Mala pinned Harper to the ground, trying to scratch at her face.

"Umbras. Creations from the other side." Cato said ducking as Allister swung his fist at him, sending Allister stumbling away. Mala glared at Cato for a moment before she felt something against her stomach, she glanced down and Harper's boots were against her, Mala's eyes widened as Harper tensed her legs, pushing upwards and throwing Mala clear.

Harper let out a sigh as Mala went sailing through the air to the ground. Once she landed, she rolled up and hissed, spit spraying from her oversized mouth. Harper didn't react just prepared herself for Mala as she scampered after her. Mala was almost on her when a bin lid smacked into the ground in front of her.

Mala swiveled to the side and glared at Tai, standing with the others as Harper ran around to stand next to Brooklyn and Lola.

The group stood together, Xander, Allister and Tai stood in front of the girls. Jia and Audrey side by side, with Brooklyn, Lola and Harper in front of them, everyone panting and exhausted. All the umbras had disappeared leaving the ground covered in ooze. Cato growled as Mala crouched down.

"It's laughable that you still don't know who you are." Mala laughed; Cato standing next to her his arms folded staring angrily at Tai.

"What are you talking about?" Audrey asked, as Xander whipped away another umbra.

"You are the reincarnates, but somehow know nothing about your powers." Mala said, as she pointed to each of them individually.

"Sagittarius, Libra, Cancer, Virgo, Aquarius, Scorpio, Taurus." Mala said.

"And Capricorn." Cato said his eyes meeting Brooklyn's. The gems began to glow at each name mentioned. Harper frowned, the umbras left and Mala smirked.

"Whatever you say, we've still stopped you at every turn." Tai snapped.

"You've just been lucky." Cato hissed.

"Mistress was right, Altair could never be trusted." Mala added, the two disappeared along with the monsters. Everyone transformed back, silence filling the air.

Chapter 18 Destiny

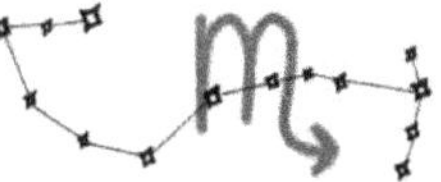

"Kumiko. We need some answers." Tai said. Kumiko glanced up from her book as the group strode into Altair Sweet Shop.

"Doesn't everyone?"

"They were talking about us being reincarnates, what do they mean by that?" Audrey asked. Kumiko stilled and closed her book.

"You know something. So tell us." Allister said. She stood up and placed her book on the table.

"Don't listen to them." Kumiko replied, turning away from the group.

"Are we just being used by you?" Brooklyn asked. Kumiko didn't respond. "Kumiko?"

"You are our destiny." And she walked out of Altair.

Jia was laid on her bed, her foot tapping to the beat of her music as she drew in her art book. Nothing ever fazed her and truthfully, she was enjoying her life right now. The excitement, the new friends that she never thought she'd have, the magic. She lifted her palm and brushed the rubber dustings off her desk.

A big grin appeared on her lips before she continued drawing once more. Even though it was fun there was an air of danger with it all; she was worried about her friends getting hurt, or her family.

She wondered if there was more she could do but every time they brought it up with Kumiko, she'd give no answer or disappear for days on end. She felt a wave of tiredness wash over her. She began to pack away her things and settle down for the night.

"Maybe there is an answer in my dreams?" she thought as she switched off her lamp and snuggled into her bed with her favourite plush nestled against her chest.

"Happy Halloween!" Allister and Jia yelled. Brooklyn's eyes widened in panic, and she shoved the two back.

"What are you doing?" Lola snapped. Following behind the startled Brooklyn, Allister and Jia smiled sheepishly.

"Getting ready for a spooky week!" Allister cheered; Lola shook her head as Brooklyn turned to her.

"What's happening?" she asked. Jia sat down on the ground and stared up at the group.

"Every year our school hosts a week long Halloween festival. With the final day being on Halloween, with a big party, some cool games and things like that." She explained excitedly. Allister nodded.

"And then we all go to the cemetery for after-hour activities." he said squeezing Lola's sides making her jump.

"Do you?" Jia and Brooklyn asked together, one confused and the other in awe. Allister laughed and ruffled Jia's head.

"That's right, you're not in our year."

"Or part of the cool group." Audrey teased. Lola sighed as she picked up her bag, glanced around the room and frowned before turning to the group.

"Well, you all have fun with that, I have to go." She said before walking off as the bell rang, Brooklyn held out her hands and Jia gripped them as Brooklyn pulled her up. Allister pushed the two girls forward as Audrey waved them off in a different direction.

"I'll see you guys after school! Halloween is a go!" she called punching the air with her fist before running off out of the courtyard.

Jia, Brooklyn and Allister made it just in time for English as they sat together at a table as the teacher walked in. Brooklyn stared after them as they placed their folder on the front desk. This woman had her platinum white hair pulled back into a low bun, with two tendrils framing her face, her glasses bold and round highlighting the grey flecks in her pale blue eyes.

"Good morning. As you know Halloween is just around the corner and in your form groups you will be deciding upon your Halloween contribution." she announced, glancing around the room as everyone began to cheer, especially Allister and Jia. "Along with this, the Halloween Bash will be held on the Saturday evening this year." she added before pulling out a slip of paper and passing it around the room. "Don't forget to vote for what your head boy and girl will be wearing for the week. Any questions?"

Everyone began to chatter, writing on pieces of paper and discussing ideas. Brooklyn leant over to Jia, as she was given a piece of paper.

"Who is head girl and boy?" She asked, Jia smiled knowingly and held up her piece of paper, in swirls of pink flowers and golden roses covering the edges, Harper's name was centre of the paper with demon priestess underneath. Brooklyn's eyes widened in surprise as she glanced around the room before back at Jia.

"Harper's head girl? How?" She laughed and Jia smiled in return as she began writing on the second piece of paper.

"She's pretty smart, pretty cool, pretty helpful. Pretty, pretty." Jia babbled; Brooklyn smiled, nodding as she wrote down a costume idea of her own for Harper. With the teacher yelling orders the students began handing in their pieces of paper before returning to their seats ready to start what was left of the lesson. Brooklyn walked up the aisle with Jia's and her paper, when a student popped her hand up.

"Mrs. Huxley, do you know whether the ghost is going to interfere with the Halloween bash?"

Brooklyn narrowed her eyes and stared at the student, as their teacher took her papers.

"I shouldn't think so. It's just silly rumours in line with Halloween, nothing more, nothing less." Mrs. Huxley answered, dismissing Brooklyn who hurried back to her seat. Allister leant forward to her,

"You thinking what I'm thinking?" he whispered. She nodded in response.

"Allister, back in your seat." she snapped. He gave an uncomfortable laugh as a couple of boys in the class sniggered and ooh'd. Brooklyn rolled her eyes as everyone turned to the board.

"Shakespeare's journey began with his first play…" She began to write along the board as Jia, Brooklyn and Allister watched the clock waiting for the end of the lesson.

The group had split up for the next session, Brooklyn had caught up with Lola ready for cooking.

"Five flour packs. Three dye sets." Brooklyn checked off the list as Lola picked up the items and put them in the bag.

"Are we done yet?" Lola asked. Brooklyn gave a small smile, knowing full well patience was not Lola's specialty.

"Almost. Are you looking forward to Halloween?" she asked as Lola stepped off the step ladder.

"It's the same every year." she huffed. As they began to walk out they heard a shatter and they stopped.

"What was that?" Lola asked, stepping her back into Brooklyn. The noise happened again, closer this time.

"It's the ghost." Brooklyn said. Lola shook her head.

"There's no such thing."

"I mean… really?" Brooklyn responded. As quick as a flash the top shelf of pots fell off one after the other, clattering around the two girls causing them to scream. They dropped the ingredients and ran to the door. As soon as they were out, they ran into Tai's arms, startling him as he was walking by.

"The ghost!" Brooklyn squeaked as Tai tightened his grip around them. Lola turned slightly looking back at the door, she squinted harder, a pair of golden eyes staring back at her before they disappeared. She was about to speak when she realized the commotion they caused had created a crowd around them, the whispering starting. Brooklyn lowered her head trying to ignore it all, her chest feeling tight. Lola glanced up at Tai and stepped back slightly.

It isn't real right?" she asked lowering her voice. Tai shrugged his shoulders.

"Or it's, them?" he whispered.

"What is going on here?" a man with bright orange hair yelled, the crowd moved aside and the trio kept quiet. "Well?" He said again, tapping his foot impatiently.

"They saw the ghost Mr. Ford!" a student shouted, causing everyone to chatter amongst themselves. Mr. Ford stormed forward, and Brooklyn, Tai and Lola looked up at him.

"Explain now." he demanded. Lola pursed her lips together and Mr. Ford's brown eyes narrowed to Tai. "Tai. What happened?"

Tai squeezed Brooklyn's hip and rubbed Lola's arm before stepping through the pair of them.

"It was an accident. Nothing happened." he explained. Mr. Ford eyed him and the two girls standing behind him.

"Brooklyn right?" Mr. Ford said, Brooklyn nodding as he continued to scrutinize her. "Very well." He turned to everyone. "Get back to class now." he ordered as he walked away and the crowd dispersed. Lola and Tai sighed, Brooklyn stared at them.

"You don't think it's one of those shadow creatures?" She asked, the two shrugged, heading back to class without the ingredients.

Jia was sitting on the bench when she heard her name being called. She glanced up from her book and saw Allister jogging over to her.

"Hey watcha doing out here?" he asked. Jia smiled slightly.

"I was just deciding if I wanted to go to class… I just feel odd today." she explained, Allister nodded and held out his hand, she stared at it before taking his hand and he pulled her up.

"Come on I'll walk you and you can tell me all about it." He grinned and Jia nodded and the two walked to their next class. As they went, Jia explained about her drawings and dreams recently when they heard a group of girls laughing together. Jia stared at them and Allister glanced across at her, as the girls looked at the pair and began to laugh louder. Jia frowned and bent down going into her bag, Allister scowled slightly before placing his hand on her shoulder.

"Hey don't listen to them, they… Jia?" He stopped talking as she pulled out her doodle book, opened it and held it up for Allister.

"I… have a bad feeling…" she stammered. Allister stared at it and up to where the picture replicated. His eyes widened and he ran past Jia, she watched him go and he rugby tackled the girl laughing the loudest. Jia watched as the girl was tackled to the ground, and the sound of shattering filled the courtyard.

The girls were now screaming in fear as Allister hit the ground with the girl wrapped in his arms, protectively cradling her head from hitting the ground. Jia put her book away and ran over, helping the girls step away from the broken plant pot. Footsteps could be heard, Allister let go of the girl and she stared at him, her cheeks reddening, her eyes watering.

"Thank you Allister." she muttered. Allister sat up as Jia pulled the girl to her feet.

"Don't worry about it."

She headed to her friends and burst into tears.

"The ghost tried to kill me!" she wailed, the head teacher, hearing the commotion, could be seen running over from the main building, where she slowed down as she heard the wailing. Jia rubbed her temple.

"There is no such thing as ghosts. You all should be in class! Who made this mess?" Mrs. Fornem, their tired eyed head teacher said glaring at the kids, as Jia and Allister exchanged looks. The group of girls protested and began blaming the ghosts.

"Jia! What are you doing out here? Allister, you too? Get to class. Girls, please stop crying, no one was hurt." Mrs. Fornem snapped and ushered the girls to their class, all the while still complaining that it was the ghost. Jia and Allister looked up to where the plant pot should have been, Allister rubbing his head and dusting off his trousers.

"You know, whatever it is about your painting, that was a life saver." he said. Jia gave a small smile, unsure to believe him or not. "Right come on. I'll walk you to class and then I'm gonna get this looked at." he mused, holding up his bloody arm. Jia's eyes widened and she grabbed his arm causing him to hiss.

"Sorry! Are you okay?"

"I'll be fine. Come on." he said taking her by the arm and dragging her along. She glanced back at the broken pot as the caretaker came along, Jia's eyes narrowed as she glanced up to the roof, a distant shadow disappearing behind it.

"Surely I would have drawn a ghost too?" she thought as she was led away for the final session of the day.

The next day, everyone had begun to decorate the school for the Halloween bash.

"Day two!" Jia cheered, as she hopped up the steps to the school; skeletons were climbing out of the ground, hanging pumpkin lanterns were attached to the trees, swinging softly in the cool breeze. Cobwebs filled the windows, and several bushes had bats covering them pulsing with a red glow.

"Apart from the first day being filled with ghoulish activities, it's been a pretty fun time." Brooklyn said, hobbling up the steps with Jia, a new habit the two had fallen into over the last month since Brooklyn joined Silver Valley.

The two were heading towards the dance and drama block to Art class when they both heard swearing. They exchanged glances and headed for the dance studio to find Audrey and her dancers.

"Are you kidding me!?" Audrey screamed, staring at the ripped and clawed costumes. Brooklyn and Jia stood behind Audrey, and Harper appeared next to them, as the dance group stood devastated.

"Who did this?" one of the dancers said. Everyone just glanced around as Brooklyn poked Harper's back.

"The ghost..." she whispered. Audrey glanced back and scowled.

"It's not." She bit her tongue and stared back at the costumes, before placing her hand on her face and sighed.

"Alrighty. We're just gonna have to work overtime." Audrey declared, the girls groaning and Audrey growling in annoyance. She turned to Harper, Jia and Brooklyn, and grabbed their hands dragging them to her height.

"I won't be able to help for the next few days until this is sorted. I'm sorry, but… dance is…" She trailed off, Brooklyn smiled softly and pulled her in for a hug.

"Don't worry, dance is everything for you. We'll cover for you if they show up." she said, Harper nodded in agreement. They heard footsteps and a small, bright starry-eyed woman walked in, however her bright eyes dwindled as she gawked at the sight in front of her.

"What happened?" she asked. Audrey stepped forward.

"We're not sure Miss Adair, but we'll figure it out." she answered confidently. Harper sighed and crossed her arms over her chest as she watched the teacher walk around with students close on her heels.

"I'm getting sick of this. This week is turning into a nightmare." she murmured, Brooklyn nodding in agreement.

"The ghost ruined our work!" a student declared. Miss Adair rolled her eyes,

"There is-"

Brooklyn, Harper and Audrey joined in with the teacher's declaration.

"No such thing as ghosts!"

"Go to class girls, I'm sure it's just the final years pulling unnecessary pranks. I'll see you all later." Miss Adair whispered sadly ushering them out. Something caught the corner of Brooklyn's eyes and she stopped, turning slightly, a black sliver ducking under the open window.

She frowned and took a step forward, however Miss Adair cleared her throat, Brooklyn glanced at her and chuckled uncomfortably as Miss Adair tapped her foot waiting, and Brooklyn joined the others as they trailed out of the studio.

The day before Halloween, the ghost had been getting creative and causing more havoc in the school, causing concern to students, parents and teachers alike. Rumors were circling that they would cancel the Bash for fear that something deadly could occur.

"This week has been ridiculous." Allister said, as he sat down on the grass. Jia swung back and forth on the swings as Brooklyn sat still on her swing. Tai was leant against the tree as Lola and Harper were sitting on the bench and Xander walked up, drink in hand.

"You should be so lucky to not be at school." Jia moaned. Xander stopped by Tai and offered him his drink, Tai took it from him.

"What is wrong with being at school?" Xander asked directing his question to Harper as Tai took a gulp of the drink, instantly regretting it.

"The 'ghost' has ruined yet another Halloween activity." she explained. Lola gestured around.

"Hence no Audrey today." she said. Xander took back his drink as Tai slowly lowered to the ground, his hand covering his mouth as he gagged, causing Brooklyn to smile and Allister to laugh.

"It's not a ghost."

"That's what we've all said but it's getting a bit hard to believe it because no one can see 'it'. 'It' just happens and they're getting worse." Lola sighed. Xander thought for a moment, sipping on his straw.

"What if we staked it out? On Halloween?" he suggested. The group all exchanged looks thinking about this for a moment. Jia jumped off the swing and punched the air excitedly.

"Let's do it!"

"Let's catch us a ghost." Allister piped up. Lola groaned but stood up.

"I don't want it ruining the Halloween bash."

Harper stood up along with Brooklyn.

"Alright and if it turns out to be Cato and Mala, we'll be ready." she said. Everyone nodded in agreement and began to head out of the park, a sense of justice coursing through their veins as Tai still sat on the ground.

"What was in that drink?" he whined, closing his eyes in disgust.

Chapter 19 Uncanny

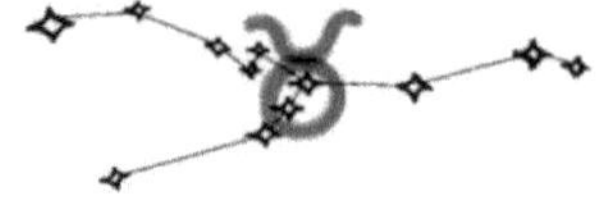

"Stop wriggling Jia."

"Shh, someone will hear us."

"Move over. I can't breathe!"

"That's it! I've had enough!"

Lola burst through the door and the others fell forward in a pile of tangled limbs, groaning and yelping at each other. Lola glanced down the darkened corridor as Xander was perched on the others sipping his drink. Jia slowly dragged her way out of the pile as Audrey rolled off. Tai winced a little and his eyes opened to see Brooklyn on top of him, her eyes shut and her hair cascading around her face.

"Uh Brooke." he said, as Allister kneed him forcing Tai to groan and Brooklyn opened her eyes.

"Sorry!" she said. Tai lay still and chuckled uncomfortably.

"Don't worry about it." He pushed himself up onto his elbows as Brooklyn sat up, finally everyone was off them. Brooklyn felt her cheeks burning and she glanced away.

"Would you two hurry up." Lola snapped. The two blushed harder and they scrambled to their feet, earning amused looks from

Audrey and Allister. Harper turned on the flashlight and they began their walk down the corridors of the quiet school.

"I'm so excited!" Audrey jumped up and down as they opened and closed another door.

"Why?" Lola asked, as she peered into the locked science room, searching for any sign of the 'ghost.'

"Because they messed with my dance, now I mess with them." She cackled. Brooklyn laughed and Lola shook her head.

"I'm surrounded by morons." she moaned as Xander held up his hand and Harper pointed down the corridor of the science and history building. They all stopped their chatter and concentrated. A low howl came from the end of the corridor and a shadow disappeared down the steps.

"It's coming from the basement." Jia's teeth chattered as she grabbed Lola's arm. Brooklyn was breathing heavily hiding behind Tai's back as Allister flickered the torch to down the stairs. Xander adjusted his glasses and he and Harper began walking down the steps with the others behind them.

As they reached the bottom of the stairs, Tai reached for a light switch, but nothing turned on.

"Oh that's less fun." Jia mumbled, still gripping Lola's arm. Xander slowly moved the torch across the basement; it was full with broken chairs and boards.

Dust covered boxes that had never been open. Pots and pans precariously balancing on a table. They all took a step down the creaking stairs, each step bringing them closer to the pitter patter of noise.

"Should we split up and search?" Tai suggested, earning several "no's". Allister ran his hand along the boxes, and he knocked one over. Everyone jumped and he chuckled.

"Sorry guys that was me."

Harper and Xander kept moving as everyone ducked and peered into every nook and cranny of the place.

"This is hopeless. There's nothing here." Lola hissed heading back towards the aisle of tables. They all heard a thud, and they froze. They glanced around every which way. Then the scratching started, and Lola and Brooklyn screamed gripping each other as Allister swung the flashlight behind him, to see a box moving towards them.

Audrey jumped up onto Tai's back and squealed as everyone began running as the box chased them, erratically moving from side to side. Xander, perfectly composed, stared at the box from the side lines as the others were running up and down the aisles trying to escape the box.

Suddenly it stopped and the group stopped moving, staring at it. Xander moved towards it and the box flung open, Allister let out a squeal and everyone turned to him, as Xander put his hand in the box and pulled out a tiny feral

"Cat!?" Everyone yelled in disbelief. It blinked and hissed raising its claws and tried to reach for Allister's face. Xander pulled it back slightly and it growled flicking its tail.

"What do we do with it?" Audrey asked, all her simmering anger disappearing as she stared lovingly at the cat.

"Leave it?" Lola said, folding her arms over her chest.

"How cruel." Tai placed his hands on Lola's shoulders and gave her a shake; she let him and huffed in disapproval. Harper stepped forward and cleared her throat.

"We should at least put it out of the school grounds, it's probably stuck in here and no one knows about it." she instructed. The group nodded in agreement and Xander placed the cat back in the box much to its protest and he closed the lid as Brooklyn very carefully made some holes, so it could breathe.

"All's well and ends well!" Jia laughed jumping onto Brooklyn's back. Lola nodded pushing open the door.

"That's not the quote." she said. Audrey laughed as Jia blushed. "Some genius." she joked.

"At least it's finally over." Harper said as Xander put the box down, outside the school front doors. Allister stretched his arms above his head.

"Who would have thought it was just a cat!" he exclaimed, as Harper sighed, pulling up her jacket closer as the cold air hit them all. Xander gave a small shrug of his shoulders.

"It could have been worse."

"At least it's over! I got my revenge." Audrey cackled. Lola raised her eyebrow and was about to speak when Tai stopped.

"No it's not over." He pointed his finger out slightly in front of him and everyone turned to follow his gaze to see several unhappy faces.

"Oh damn." Allister muttered.

Chapter 20 Extraordinary

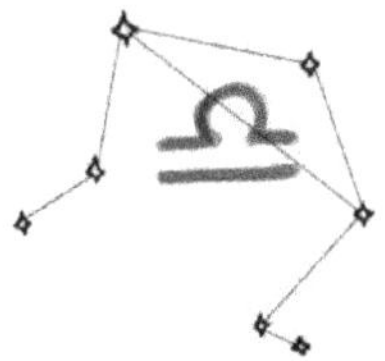

Brooklyn stared at her disappointed father as Jia lowered her head in apology. Allister's mum was pacing back and forth as Tai's father and Audrey's mother were staring at the cat in Xander's box.

"What a way to meet parents huh?" Tai whispered to Brooklyn who gave a slight tilt of her head in acknowledgement.

"So, you're telling me. That this 'sleepover' was so that you can break into school?" Jia's mother snapped; Jia flinched.

"No… it was to save a cat." she insisted, as Allister's mum stopped and turned to the group.

"I thought you'd grown out of this?" she asked Allister who shrugged his shoulders.

"No one got hurt."

"It's the trust you broke." Brooklyn's dad answered, earning nods from the parents. Lola, Xander and Harper just exchanged looks, keeping quiet.

"I suppose we'll take the cat to the shelter in the morning." Audrey's mum finally spoke up and Tai's dad turned to Brooklyn and Tai.

"You're grounded."

Tai's jaw tightened and Brooklyn lowered her gaze.

"Who organised this?" her dad asked, receiving no response. The parents sighed.

"It is late, we need to be getting home. But this will be the last time we catch you all doing something like this." Jia's mum ordered. Reluctantly everyone nodded and Tai's dad glanced at Lola, Harper and Xander.

"Uh.. we will drop you home along the way." he said as the others slowly disappeared, the parents apologising to other parents for their child's behaviour.

"Dad." Brooklyn began, however Xander spoke up.

"I will take these two home. Sorry for the trouble we caused." he said and pulled Lola and Harper by their hands leaving Brooklyn and her father.

"Brooklyn. Really?" he said, his eyes narrowing as Brooklyn clenched her fists.

"It wasn't like we were wrecking the school. Or doing anything of…" She trailed off as her father began walking away.

"Last chance Brooklyn, please. Your mother is tired of it." he said softly, and it took all of Brooklyn's willpower to not burst into tears.

The next few days the group had kept a low profile. Audrey had filled them in about the cat and it was doing much better now that it was safe and eating properly, they had named it Ghost which she thought was fitting. Their parents had mostly forgiven the group and had called it a one off and Halloween hijinks.

However, they were on their best behaviour leading up to the Halloween Bash and it would appear that Cato and Mala were too. Everyone had gathered in the gymnasium having dressed up in costume. Allister wore a Captain Jack Sparrow outfit, several students had come along in group costumes, with a collection of Spider-man, Deadpool and Black Widows.

Jia had dressed as Doctor Who, with a fully functioning screwdriver that glowed. Teachers had joined in the fun with all wearing Alice in Wonderland character costumes, Brooklyn laughed as she spotted her PE teacher as White Rabbit. She spotted Tai and he waved to her wearing a Frankenstein monster costume.

Lola was currently by the DJ, her red straightened hair easy to spot from where Brooklyn was standing in her Sally costume.

"You enjoying your first Halloween bash?" Harper asked as she placed a drink against Brooklyn's arm.

"Oh!" Brooklyn jumped at the cool touch and glanced up at Harper wearing a Day of the Dead costume, her purple hair tightly curled, her face covered with black and purple stitches and flowers, wearing a glittering black ruffled organza gothic skirt and a dark purple corset which shimmered with every movement and three large black and purple flowers adorning her shoulder and finished off with a black spiky crown on her head.

Brooklyn took the drink from her. "Yeah!" she answered, as she glanced back at the party, people watching. Harper nodded and leant against the wall, breathing in deeply the fresh scent of cinnamon candles and toffee apples.

"At least my last one is extraordinary." She mused sipping her apple cider. Brooklyn snapped her attention away from the dancing students and a small pout replaced her smile.

"Oh right, this is your last year." she murmured. Harper chuckled and nudged Brooklyn's shoulder.

"It's not like this year will be the last you see me. Not with everything else going on." She rotated her wrist and gestured around to the people that were now Brooklyn's friends. Jia was apple bobbing, Audrey was on the stage in a skeleton outfit performing a spooky

Halloween dance with her dance group, before teaching younger students as she went. Allister was amidst a battle at wrapping another student up in toilet paper and Tai was talking with a group of girls and Lola on the dance floor.

"I guess that's true." she said sipping her own lemonade, the bubbles tingling the back of her throat. Harper gave a small nod and the two stood in comfortable silence, watching the world go by.

Down in the depths of the basement Cato and Mala were skulking around.

"Could you be any louder?" Cato muttered; Mala was staring up at the ceiling growling at the bass vibrating through the floor.

"It's just so boring. Why can't we attack that?" she asked pointing to the ceiling, Cato turned around to her and rolled his eyes as he ducked down and scanned the floor. Mala took a step forward her eyes still on the ceiling.

"You... damn it!" She yelled as she fell headfirst over Cato's back. He straightened up and frowned at her.

"Shut up." he hissed as Mala sprawled out in front of him, he could hear her growling and cursing as he crawled forward until he spotted a dim glowing light.

"Found you." he said reaching forward. From behind the clutter and filth of the basement the light grew more prominent, his eyes blazed in the light as he took the item.

"I hope you're ready, Brooklyn. This fight is ours." And they vanished into nothingness.

Chapter 21 Frenemy

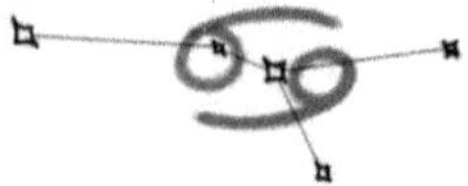

A few weeks had passed since the Halloween bash and they were in the deep thrall of winter, with the days short and the nights long and the crisp. Winter air was threatening all. The whole of Silver Valley were immersed in Christmas decorations and shopping for the upcoming Christmas Day.

During that time, the glowing item that Cato and Mala had found. Seemed to have lost some of its power so the pair were biding their time in the quiet of their abandoned silver mine. Though today, Cato had found himself staring at a screen through the window of a small shop, his forehead creasing in concentration.

He had been standing there for an hour watching this screen with people in it, unaware of people staring at him with confused and wary eyes. He had grown to understand that, if the creatures in the screen were truthful, it seemed attacking the enemy directly would never work. He hummed softly in thought; he had to find a different way.

"Uh excuse me sir, but you're scaring our customers." A small elderly man stepped out of the front door a small smile on his wrinkled face. Cato turned to him and raised an eyebrow before huffing. Cato gave a small grin, his teeth sharpening and his eyes and ears growing bigger.

He watched as the man's eyes began to widen in fear and as quickly as he appeared, disappeared back into the shop closing the blinds swiftly. Cato laughed and began his smug return to the mining tunnel. Once he arrived back to his new home Mala greeted him with a yawn and swish of her tail. He ducked out of the way and continued to lay down on the ground, thinking.

"What's the matter with you?" Mala said, never opening her eyes.

"None of your business."

"Fine."

"I'm thinking of a new plan."

"Don't care."

Cato sighed and closed his eyes, resting his hand over his forehead, he let the silence calm his thoughts.

"I've got it!" Cato sat bolt upright, Mala jumped and fell off the rock her eyes wide awake.

"What?"

"I have a plan! After watching that screen it's simple! I attack the family!" he declared. Mala frowned climbing back onto her perch and curled up in a ball.

"Whatever you say."

Cato stood up and began walking to the entrance of the tunnel once more.

"Don't wreck the place whilst I'm gone!" he yelled. He was answered with a loud snort of derision.

Cato stared at the little girl tapping her foot against the ground, an unhappy pout on her face. He rested his chin on his palm and grinned, the little girl began to huff and puff before turning around and moving back towards the gates.

He had seen through his monsters, this little girl had been with Brooklyn before, when they first arrived in this city. Surely they were connected, with the way Brooklyn held her hand and coddled her. He jumped down from atop the building he was perched on and began to walk towards the little girl.

He had one chance to make sure this worked, he slowed his thoughts and closed his eyes as he watched back through the umbras eyes. His focus went to Brooklyn, echoes of her calling her friends' names, the shock of seeing the umbra for the first time, the running through the streets. He filtered through until he found voices of the little girl.

"Okay, Kay, I need you to trust your big sister…"

Cato exhaled, further. He needed just a little more.

"Hi I'm Kayleigh!"

"Kayleigh?" he questioned smiling brightly, stopping by the gate. The little girl turned around and gave him a disgusted look.

"Who are you?"

Cato raised his arms in surrender, keeping the smile on his face.

"Cato. I'm a friend of your sister. Brooklyn." he offered. The little girl's eyes narrowed.

"You're nothing like that guy Tai." she sniffed. The cloud rolled overhead and she glanced up at them. "No, I don't want it to rain." she whined Cato was amused and confused by the little girl but he continued on.

"Your sister is running late, I offered to collect you and take you home." he said. Kayleigh again wrinkled her nose up.

"But… you're not handsome like Tai." she cooed, thinking of Tai. Cato scowled.

"You're testing my patience kid." he ground out. Kayleigh puffed out her cheeks and folded her arms over her chest.

"Go away! I don't like guys like you!"

Cato's eyes widened and he held up his hands and began shaking them.

"Look I'm sorry! I'll behave." he said, clearly bewildered by the young brunette and she side-eyed him before nodding in approval.

"Fine, but no funny business mister." She took his hand and dragged him along the streets, heading for her house.

"I don't know why mummy and daddy think I can't do this walk by myself. I'm very smart. Unlike Brooklyn, she gets caught sneaking out, and not doing chores." Kayleigh began rambling away as Cato's frown deepened with every passing second. "I just bat my eyelashes and Daddy or Cal do things for me."

"So you're a… you're a harpie?" he asked. Kayleigh glanced up at him, her head tilting in confusion.

"What's that?"

"A creature with wings and talons, known for manipulating mortals." he answered. She blinked a few times, shrugged and continued on her rant.

"Oh! And at school our teacher is so selfish we only got ten minutes of reading time! I could have read for longer but no, some of my classmates would not be quiet." She sighed and wistfully asked "why can't everyone be more like Tai?" Cato yanked Kayleigh to a stop as they came to a set of lights, he had seen several people crossing at these things when the light is green. Kayleigh stared at him and grinned,

"Thank you." She beamed and he wrinkled his nose up in disgust. They crossed the road together and Kayleigh was still talking as Cato glanced up at the sky, the rain hadn't fallen but the clouds were darkening, and the sun was lowering to behind the taller buildings in the distance.

"Cato!"

He realised they had stopped walking and he stared down at the pouting girl.

"I'm home." she said matter-of-factly. His jaw dropped and his eyes widened, she had opened the door and was swinging on her heels back and forth. "Thanks. Well see ya!" She waved him goodbye, and Cato watched as the door slammed shut on him. He blinked a few times, really walking through his plan in his head before he clenched his fists. He'd been outsmarted by a kid! He raked his claws through his hair and stomped away.

"Fine. I'll just scare her instead." He knew it wouldn't take long for Brooklyn to come looking for him now that her little sister was part of his game. He perched himself up against a tree and waited. "Why go hunting when you can just wait for your prey to come to you."

The group had gathered once more in the city library, Lola stood at the front of the table pacing. Halloween was over and school was a little dull now, all the scary and unusual decorations had disappeared and the 'ghost' a distant memory.

Boxes of every size filled the library as everyone was getting ready for the Christmas decorations. Brooklyn was staring down at her phone; her parents had been messaging her. Reminding her about Kayleigh, making sure she was safe, asking her where she was, reminding her not to be late.

She pursed her lips and pushed the buttons texting out her response, a slight rush of heat running through her body and settling uncomfortably in her chest.

"Hello? Earth to the new girl!" Lola flicked Brooklyn in the forehead causing the brunette to jump in her seat.

"Sorry, what?" she mumbled out. Lola rolled her eyes and huffed as she continued walking around. Everyone stared at Brooklyn and she felt her cheeks redden.

"I was saying, after days and days of Cato and Mala harassing us, to be polite, they've gone silent. Which can only really mean the worst. So my question was, what do we do?" Lola snapped, Brooklyn glanced around everyone shrugged or glanced around.

"Why don't we just hold off till something happens?" she suggested causing Lola to stop.

"After you all said we need to be on alert?"

"It might be a good sign, maybe they've gotten bored." Brooklyn responded.

"Mala does seem like the type." Allister piped up, Lola sat down and drummed her purple nails on the table, the sparkles glinting in the light every time her nails clipped the table.

"After Halloween, I have to say my parents are on me." Brooklyn said stiffly, Audrey nodded her head in agreement.

"Yeah Lola, it's been difficult getting out of the house without getting the third degree." She added. Tai tapped his finger on the desk and nodded as Allister piped up.

"But we can get through this." he said cheerfully. Lola flicked her wrist to him.

"See, some commitment."

Xander, Jia and Harper were sitting in silence watching the group curiously. Brooklyn sighed.

"Lola, I think we just all need to take a break for a bit." she suggested. Lola scoffed.

"Oh right, now you want to 'take a break' after your whole, 'yeah magic!' 'Yeah let's do it!' 'Yeah Lola it's amazing." she mimicked, Brooklyn scowling in response.

"What?" she ground out. Tai raised his hand as Lola leant over the table towards Brooklyn.

"Come on guys."

"You heard me. You were all for it to begin with. Get in a little trouble and now it's 'oh woe is me, we need to stop'…" Lola stopped as Brooklyn slammed her hands on the table and stood up.

"Fine! Be like that!" she yelled and stormed out of the library, ignoring the disapproving glances from the librarians, heading home. Her anger simmering slightly as she noticed park goers jogging, having picnics, enjoying a quiet evening as the sun sets.

She pulled her collar up as a cool breeze blew past her, it wasn't meant to be like this.

She thought, honestly, that she would have lived a quiet life, stay out of trouble, make maybe a few good friends, friends who wouldn't just ditch her the moment she was told she was moving. She sighed as she jimmied the key in the door and entered her house. She took off her jacket and shoes and went to the sofa and turned on the tv. She sighed and closed her eyes, before flopping onto her side, burying her face into the pillow.

Maybe she was a bit harsh but all of this was too much for her. She felt herself slowly slip into a slumber, her exhausted mind and body relaxing finally.

The darkness surrounded her but for one small little light.

"Brooklyn…"

"I can't do this." she whispered, the glow hummed softly, the light bathing her in warmth.

"You can and you will get through this. You do not need to burden yourself, your friends will be there for you." The Light said softly, *"I know it can be scary, but you were chosen for a reason."*

"How can you be so sure? We barely know each other." Brooklyn said in frustration.

"This is what you were born to do. Believe in yourself." The light began to flicker. Brooklyn's eyes widened and she shot her hand out.

"No please don't go!" she yelled. The light disappeared leaving Brooklyn alone in the darkness.

"Brooke?" A voice awoke her from her slumber, and she rubbed her eyes before opening them to see her brother looming over her. She sat up, and frowned, a blanket having been placed over her. She held onto it and wrapped herself in it as Cal rubbed his hand over his face.

"What are you doing here?" she asked. He sat down next to her and she pulled her legs up, narrowly missing getting sat on.

"I finished my shift early tonight. You rarely sleep on the sofa, what's wrong?" He asked with a heaviness to his voice.

"I had an argument with one of the girls." She explained, Cal nodded.

"Where's Kayleigh? Is she in her room? Mum and dad are working till very late tonight so I'll cook us dinner." he said. Brooklyn's eyes widened, she'd forgotten her sister. She scrambled out of her chair and grabbed her phone, her brother opening his eyes at the commotion. Brooklyn grabbed her shoes and headed for the door when the door from upstairs opened, Cal and Brooklyn looked up and Kayleigh stood at the top of the stairs. Brooklyn exhaled shakily,

"I'm sorry!" She breathed out and Kayleigh tilted her head to the side and frowned.

"Why? Your friend picked me up from school."

"What?!" Cal almost yelled and Brooklyn flinched. Kayleigh bounded down the stairs and into Cal's arms. He lifted her up and stared at Brooklyn.

"So you're telling me, you forgot your sister? And slept on the sofa? And your friend just happened to pick her up?" He sounded out every word, annoyance in his voice. Brooklyn took off her shoes and nodded.

"Who was your friend?" he added. Brooklyn stared at her phone, she hadn't received any messages.

"Cato." Kayleigh said. Cal frowned and slowly turned to Brooklyn; the colour in her cheeks disappeared and her lips began to tremble, Kayleigh tilted her head to the side.

"What?" Brooklyn whispered, Cal tightened his grip on his younger sister, eyes narrowing and Brooklyn brought her hands up to her head gripping her hair in panic.

"He said you were busy, and you'd asked him to. He was really nice to me. Bit weird though." Kayleigh explained, Cal watched his sister as she breathed out.

"Kayleigh, unless it's your sister picking you up do not go with anyone else." Cal said sternly, Brooklyn stared at her little sister.

"Okay, am I in trouble?" She asked, glancing between her two older siblings. Cal shook his head.

"No you're not. Just be more careful. Only ask for Brooklyn." he instructed, ruffling the top of her head and placing her down.

"Now get ready for dinner." She scampered off and Cal turned to Brooklyn.

"Is he your friend?"

Brooklyn opened her mouth to speak before shutting her mouth.

"I'll be back." She said and ran towards the door.

"Brooklyn!" Cal yelled, she flinched and stopped.

"Yeah, he's fine." she said softly, the lie burning her on the inside, guilt twisting around her stomach, before opening the door. She ran down the street heading straight to the docks.

"Cato!" she screamed,

"You yelled?" Cato appeared suddenly and Brooklyn turned around.

"How dare you go near my sister!" Brooklyn brought up her fist and tried to punch Cato, who took a step to the side.

"It got you here didn't it?"

"What?" Brooklyn stopped and Cato stepped closer to her,

"Let's make a deal. I can sense your fear, and you should be scared." he said, holding out his hand. "Give me your gem and your sister won't be harmed." Cato said, Brooklyn's eyes widened and her fingers brushed the velvet band around her neck before gripping her gem.

"No… but she was fine…" Brooklyn shut her eyes and Cato stared at her, she couldn't read him, he could have done something to her sister, but what?. "Why?" She opened her eyes and shoved her hands against his chest. "She's a kid! She's done nothing!" she yelled, Cato frowned and stretched his fingers.

"The gem."

Brooklyn stared down at the ground, her fingers were shaking, and she stepped back, her thoughts only of her sister.

"What did you do?" she whispered. Cato didn't respond as she began to unclip her necklace his eyes widening in surprise. "I give up, you… Kayleigh can't be involved in this. I can't let that happen." she croaked, the warmth she felt with the gem around her began to fade as she held the necklace in her palm, a tear she didn't realise had fallen, dropped off her cheek. The others would be so angry with her.

"They'll hate me." she thought closing her eyes and exhaling with defeat. Cato reached forward and just as he was about to take the necklace from Brooklyn, his hand stopped, hovering over hers. Brooklyn stared up at him and Cato took a step back, his fingers brushing hers as his hand dropped to his side.

"Kayleigh is fine." he said before disappearing into the night. Brooklyn was left with her arm outstretched, her necklace ready to fall, her thoughts mingling together, as she whispered.

"What was that?"

Brooklyn did not talk about her encounter with Cato to the others and had kept out of Lola's way for a while until one Friday afternoon Lola approached Brooklyn.

"I need your help." she said. Brooklyn stared up at Lola and grimaced.

"What?"

"I need you to come shopping with me next week."

Jia slid her chair closer.

"What's this? We're talking again? Shopping? I'm in!" She grinned and Lola blinked slowly and nodded thoughtfully. Brooklyn stared at the two.

"I guess I'm forgiven?" she thought to herself, and glanced up at Lola, who was waiting for an answer.

"Oh… yeah of course Lola." she answered. Lola nodded and turned away.

"Great. Two in the afternoon at the mall on the 21st. Don't be late." She hurried away and Jia laughed.

"She can be so weird but I'm glad you guys are friends again!" she exclaimed before going back to her art work. Brooklyn blinked, thinking it through.

"We're friends?" she thought before joining Jia and continuing her art work too.

As the Christmas holiday arrived, a few of the members had left on family vacations. Brooklyn, Jia and Lola were currently at the mall, carrying bags for Lola.

"Final stop." she said. Jia slumped to her knees and whined.

"I can't keep doing this." she mumbled, Lola frowned at her, her phone began to buzz.

"I must take this, head on in and pick yourself something for Christmas. Hello, thank you for returning my call." She began walking towards the exit. Jia and Brooklyn exchanged looks,

"How did we get roped into this?" Brooklyn asked, Jia shrugged her shoulders.

"I'm surprised she even wants to buy us Christmas presents." She took Brooklyn by the hand, "come on I have my eye on some new pencils." Jia smiled as she dragged Brooklyn with her.

Cato and Mala stare down at the people in the shops.

"Why is everything so, shiny?" Mala asked staring at the flashing Christmas lights and the sparkling baubles in the gigantic tree sparkle. Cato shrugged, his eyes scanning the crowd.

"Are you sure you found a gem?" He asked, watching as some people were laughing and exchanging 'things', whilst young children took pictures with a man with a white beard.

"Humans are strange. Why does everything… sorry what?" She snapped out of her mutterings and Cato sighed, he snatched the item, the glowing purple compass from Mala and stared at the spinning pin.

"That way." he said, jumped down from the scaffolding to the lower level, Mala following. His eyes scanned the area and he stopped momentarily; Mala poked his back.

"What?"

"Nothing." he answered, turning away. "Alright, let's do this, the gem should be nearby."

Mala grinned and opened her palms. Red sparks filled both of them and she aimed one hand above her head and the other below her.

"Hah!" she yelled, and two blasts headed in different directions, Cato watched as the banner was struck above and came toppling down to the ground and the other blast destroyed the water feature. A few of the people began screaming, and Cato and Mala lowered to the ground.

"My pretties!" Mala yelled, as creatures began crawling out of the hole in the ground from below. "Let's kill them all!"

Cato watched as people began running in different directions, tripping over each other, disregarding everyone other than themselves. He rolled his eyes and a flicker of silver caught his eye. Capricorn was stood holding up fallen debris from crushing a small human, the other, floating with her violet leaves spinning around her as she moved, Aquarius helped the small human and took it away from the danger.

"Mala!"

The red head turned and grinned.

"I thought you wouldn't show up, Sagittarius. Do you like what I've done with the place?" she asked. Tai shook his head.

"You have no right to bring innocent people into whatever grudge you have against us."

"Meh." She dived forward and the two engaged in battle.

From outside the mall, Allister and Lola were watching the news reporter.

"As you can see! Creatures are descending on the mall! What is happening to our quiet city? Who would do such a horrible thing before Christmas?" One of them covered their ears as an explosion came from inside. Allister nudged Lola and they snuck around the side.

"We gotta get in there." he said, Lola nodded.

"This way. I know a secret way in." she said, "but first..." She stared up at the CCTV camera and pushed the two of them out of its way. They both nodded.

"In the middle of twilight, when stars align, make our powers shine!"

"What took you so long?" Tai huffed as he shoved another umbra out of the way as Lola and Allister appeared.

"I am not dignifying that with an answer."

"Can we focus please." Jia said mimicking Lola's voice. Jia stepped back into Lola. The trio looked over to see Tai and Brooklyn backing towards them as well.

"This is bad." Brooklyn muttered as everyone stood back to back, staring at the creatures that were descending on them all.

"Did everyone escape?" Lola asked. Tai nodded.

As far as we're aware no civilians are in here." Brooklyn answered. Jia slumped to her knees as she stared at a creature breaking through the ceiling and dropping causing a rumble to course through the grounds. Mala grinned and Cato looked bored next to her.

"Give me. Your gems." she demanded, everyone looked at Brooklyn who looked up at her with a scowl on her face. A loud crack caused everyone to look up and a bewildered Mala and Cato jumped back as an arrow sliced the floor and exploded. The light was blinding as someone jumped in front of the group, blocking them from the incoming attack.

As the light faded, a girl with ruby red hair that bounced in curls as she landed on the ground, raised her bow and began to fire, each umbra going down instantly. Cato nudged Mala.

"Our time is up." he said. Mala scoffed but nodded and the two disappeared without a trace along with the remaining umbras. Once the dust settled and the shopping centre was quiet. The girl flicked her fingers and the bow disappeared.

"We found another member!" Jia squealed in delight, breaking the silence. Brooklyn smiled and walked forward extending her hand.

"It's nice to meet you, I'm Capricorn-" but Brooklyn was cut off by the red haired woman.

"Stay out of my way." she spat, her eyes blazing with negative emotion, leaving the group dumbfounded as they watched the eighth member walk away.

PART TWO

Chapter 22 Seize

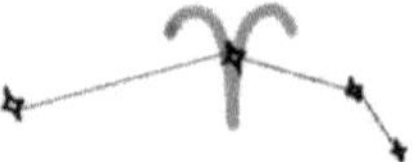

It had been three weeks since the girl with red hair had walked away from the group. Harper, Audrey and Xander had returned from their Christmas holidays, and everyone had gathered at Altair Sweet Shop.

"So, you're saying she just walked away from you?" Harper asked as she wiped down the counter. Brooklyn nodded, sweeping the floor while Lola drummed her nails on the cash register.

"It's so weird. If anything, I thought you would have avoided us." she muttered. Harper raised her eyebrow at Lola but said nothing as Xander and Kumiko walked in from the kitchen.

"Did you find out who she was?" Xander asked Jia as she held up a drawing of two sides of the same person. He leant forward, staring at the picture.

"No. We were hoping you would be able to?" Tai said. Xander placed the picture down and adjusted his glasses before sitting at the row of tables and opening his laptop.

"I can certainly try. Did she have any noticeable features? Other than the red hair." He eyed Jia as he spoke, who blushed sheepishly as she closed her mouth. Everyone began shrugging and mumbling to themselves as Xander rolled his eyes and took off his glasses, rubbing the bridge of his nose.

"Nothing? You all have nothing?" he asked as he looked round at the group. Brooklyn sighed.

"Sorry Xander."

He put his glasses back on and shook his head, tapping absently on his keyboard before standing up, closing his laptop and picking up his flask.

"I am going to need some time." he said, sipping his drink. "I will be back soon." He said as he walked through the door, leaving the others behind.

Xander walked down the streets, laptop in hand. He hadn't really thought much of this whole hero thing, but here he was. A member of the Zodiacs looking for other members, his ultimate role in this group. Was this really all he was good for? Would he have no value when everyone was found? He halted as he came to a tram stop and waited. The tram pulled up, making a familiar ping, as he got on. He sauntered to the back and stared out the window watching as the city rolled by. The glamorous city began to fade, and a darker, quieter side of the city's streets emerged. When the tram pulled to a stop, he made his way off and began his journey home. No lights were on as Xander headed inside his family's home, bounding up the stairs two at a time, he slipped to his room, closing the door with a soft click behind him. Taking a deep breath, he moved across the shadowed room towards his desk, quickly loading up his computer with practiced keystrokes, with the warm glow from the screen lighting up his face, his glasses glinting in the darkened room. The screen flickered through footage and pages, articles of mythical and mysteries until a sigh escaped Xander's lips. He leant back in his chair stretching his tired muscles, stretching his arms above his head. Closing down the tabs, leaving only the music floating gently around the room. Its soft melody making him relax into the chair, he took off his glasses and stared up at the ceiling, his eyes slowing closing.

"How did I end up in this situation?" he whispered. There was no response, no answer, no more dreams. Swivelling in his chair, Xander began to undress ready to slip into bed, stopping at the edge he thought back to the last few months, remembering that first moment of getting his gem. He had found a splendid architectural anomaly and yet when that shooting star blinded the whole of the docks, he found himself back in his room. Did his find have something to do with all this too? He sunk down onto the edge of his bed. His eyes darting to the door and he listened to his parents yelling, as they came home from wherever they had been. The words incoherent even with the shouting getting louder until a clatter of pots and pans stopped the noise. Slowly he lay down, closed his eyes, and hoped for some form of peace.

Xander jolted awake, another dream! After lying in the dark trying to work through the details in his head he finally got up and loaded up the computer. The computer seemed to hum with anticipation, almost as if it understood the gravity of the task at hand. As his fingers danced across the keyboard, the challenge felt less overwhelming, bolstered by his advanced computing skills that began to steer him forward.

After carefully reviewing the footage that Lola had sent him, Xander now looked specifically for anyone who had been around at the Docks the night of the shooting star. He traced his fingers over the keyboard, the images flickering until he spotted one image different from the others and he leant forward, squinting at the screen. A girl with a school uniform on was walking away from the cave entrance everyone else had been too. He found someone! He sat back and let out a triumphant "Yes!" He quickly opened up another tab and pulled up details on the schools around the area. He opened his notebook and began writing notes detailing which school she went to and where she can most likely be found, he smirked. Maybe he should become a detective. He reached for his phone as he set his pen down and he dialled a number, maybe he should also save the numbers of his new allies, he shook his head.

"Xander? It's late."

"Apologies, but I found the girl in red. She does not go to your school, but you might be familiar with Silvershoe Hotel. It is the daughter of the owner. I know you rarely sleep so I thought you would be the best bet. Goodnight." He hung up the phone, without waiting for a response. He dialled another number. They picked up, slower than the first number.

"Lola, I found a lead. I shall send you over the details. Goodnight." he said and hung up the phone, before he messaged Lola and went back to sleep, relaxed that he had completed his job, for now.

Laying in her bed Harper lowered her phone and stared at the address and name that appeared. She nodded to herself and put her phone away. This was it. She quietly clambered out of bed, pausing as her younger sister whined in her sleep and rolled over, her arm flopping over the edge of the bed. Grabbing her black jacket and boots Harper opened the door and snuck downstairs, carefully picked up the keys and opened the door. Holding her breath, trying not to make a sound, she stepped her foot out and slinked through the door before closing it gently behind her. Once it clicked, she began walking along the street and heading to the address she was given.

As Harper made her way up the final street, she could see the lights were still glowing bright from the hotel, residents sitting outside having quiet drinks, chatting about their day. Harper glanced around and noticed the shiny marble floor through the glass doors. A girl with bright blonde hair was leaning against the reception desk, perfectly laughing at the joke made by the receptionist, her hand placed on his shoulder before batting her eyelashes. Harper let out a huff and headed forward, the doors automatically opening as she moved closer. Harper went in and the girl retracted her hand as the receptionist cleared his throat and backed away from the girl and headed over to Harper.

"Uh, may I help you?" he asked eyeing Harper's attire. Harper raised her eyebrow and pointed to the girl behind.

"I'm here to see her. I need to have a chat."

The man turned to the girl and stepped to the side. The girl's quiet sneer quickly turned back to a sweet smile, when the man looked at her.

"Oh. Right, friend from school. I'll take it from here Oliver." She hurried past him and headed straight outside without a second glance at Harper. The man, Oliver, went back to the desk and Harper followed outside.

"So, you're Fayebelle." Harper said, as the two came to the quiet side of the pool, the blonde turning to face Harper and folding her arms over her chest.

"What can I do for you?" she mused with a slight smile. Harper leant against the railing and exhaled softly.

"I want to know why you're not helping the team?" she said. Fayebelle's eyes narrowed before they widened, and she let out a laugh.

"Oh. You are one too? That's rich." she chuckled. Harper stared at Fayebelle and Fayebelle, unfolding her arms, continued "I'm sorry but I will not be joining. I can do things by myself."

"Then you don't really understand anything at all do you." Harper cut in, as Fayebelle frowned.

"What?" she ground out.

"If you've paid any attention to what is happening, you would know you can't do it by yourself." Harper retorted. Fayebelle thought back to her dreams, had she misinterpreted them?

You are our only hope.

"Tell that to the person who called to me." she said haughtily. Harper turned around, facing the rest of Silver Valley.

"You don't understand. I thought the same way, but I was wrong, we do need you." she explained., Fayebelle let out a laugh and brushed her fingers through her hair.

"Sorry but that's not possible. I took those creatures out with ease." she bragged. Harper exhaled slowly

"Umbras."

"Whatever. Then that pair of freaks were no match either. I think you all should just sit this one out." Fayebelle answered. Harper turned around, a scowl on her face.

"You really are exactly how the media portrays you, aren't you?" she said. Fayebelle's eyes narrowed.

"What?" Fayebelle ground out as Harper began to walk away from her.

"Clearly there has been a mistake about you. You are just a spoilt, ungrateful, prissy little brat." she said. Fayebelle's eyes widened, and she spun around

"Take that back!"

"Cato and Mala can have you." Harper snapped, the scream coming from Fayebelle caused her to whip around just as the blonde lunged forward. Her body responding to the threat quickly, and she jumped to the side, Fayebelle swung at her, her fist connecting with Harper's palm. They pushed against one another until Harper pulled back her hand, causing Fayebelle to fall forward. Harper kicked her foot into the other girl's hip making her stumble clumsily to the side.

"Take it back!" she shrieked as Harper stepped away from her warily, "I would never join you!" Fayebelle snapped as she flicked her fingers and a bow and arrow appeared.

"Fine! One of our members will be without a partner and she should count herself lucky!" Harper felt her back connect with the cobbled ground of the poolside as an arrow shot past her narrowly missing her heart. Rolling to her knees Harper stared up at the blonde. "Why are you fighting in front of your hotel?!" Harper yelled.

"Like I care! Like I care about any of it!" Fayebelle barked as she fired the arrow and it shot past Harper slicing through her hair.

"I missed." Fayebelle's next arrow whizzed past Harper's head, who immediately leapt to her feet and charged towards her. Fayebelle frantically shot arrow after arrow, each one grazing harmlessly past Harper until she was within reach. With a flick of her fingers and a powerful block, Fayebelle managed to stop Harper's attack.

"I know you don't miss a shot." Harper growled, "so part of you knows what I am saying is true!"

Lola had been walking through the streets after receiving a message from Xander. He had been vague, but it was to do with Harper and the red haired girl, and that didn't sit well with her. She spotted luminescent colours coming from afar. She frowned, noticing the red from when they had met her. She ran forward, a sickening feeling washing over her.

Once she was close enough, she could see clearly that Harper and the girl were fighting. She watched as the girl fired an arrow, narrowly missing Harper. Fayebelle growled, flicked her fingers and another one appeared. Lola shook her head and ran faster.

"Stop it!" Lola yelled running towards the girls, throwing her arms out protecting Harper from the newest member.

"Lola!" Harper yelled and grabbed the younger girl, wrapping her arms around Lola, twisting so the blast of the arrow would hit her instead. However the arrow disappeared and Fayebelle lowered her bow, Lola blinked and Harper turned back around to face Fayebelle.

"You could have killed her." She hissed. Fayebelle raised an eyebrow.

"I didn't." she snapped back as she watched Lola fuss over Harper, who stared at Fayebelle.

"I don't understand why you two were fighting. I get you don't want to join us. I thought this was all ridiculous, but now I'm here… it's not… totally bad." Lola said, turning to see Fayebelle. The three stood in silence as Harper struggled to her feet, the fight taking its toll on her. Lola put her shoulder under Harper's underarm and helped her up. Fayebelle sighed.

"Fine… I can't keep avoiding you." she muttered rolling her eyes. Lola nodded slightly as the three turned away from each other. Fayebelle pulled her hair up into a high ponytail. "Get out of my hotel." she added. Harper and Lola nodded and began walking to the steps leading away from the poolside.

"Come along to Altair Sweet Shop tomorrow okay?" Lola called over her shoulder, as she and Harper left and Fayebelle returned to the hotel. Her anger boiled as she spied a group of girls chatting merrily to Oliver. Rolling her eyes Fayebelle headed to the lift and back to her room, utterly defeated for the night.

Chapter 23 Umbra

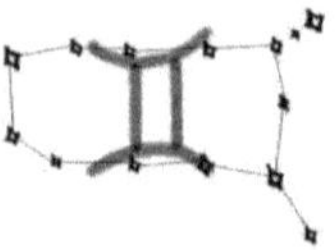

Sunday morning, everyone was hanging out at a closed Altair. Jia and Allister were in a game of stacking cups. Tai was lounging on the counter reading a text book. Xander and Brooklyn were staring at a screen. Audrey had the music playing as she swayed from side to side on the counter, her hands dancing for her. Xander had caught them all up about his call to Harper and Lola and they were waiting for them to arrive. The bell pinged and they all looked up.

"Hey guys! How are you L.A.? Harper?" Audrey said hopping off the counter. Harper acknowledged the question with a nod, arms folded with Lola close next to her.

"I told you to stop calling me that." Lola hissed with annoyance; Brooklyn frowned, however her eyes softened when she spotted a blonde behind them.

"Fayebelle Silvius?" Tai said, thinking the same thing. The blonde in front of them blushed and nodded.

"My calculation was correct Harper?" Xander asked, she nodded and gazed at Lola.

"Next time, don't tell Lola." she said and walked towards the kitchen. Lola lowered her gaze and Fayebelle rolled her eyes. Tai clapped his hands together and announced.

"Alright, we're getting there. Xander and I have a lead to follow for another member so we'll catch you guys later." He put his textbook down and began to jog out of the room. Xander nodded following along while taking a long sip of his drink. Allister yawned loudly and stood up making his way to the door.

"Well as fun as this is, I gotta go."

"Where?" Brooklyn asked, Allister tapped his nose, secretively.

"I have things to do."

"What things?" Audrey questioned. Without answering, Allister opened the door and waved back at the girls.

"See you all later." And he was gone. The girls all sat uncomfortably for a while until Jia piped up.

"Anyone know if Kumiko is coming back today?"

Everyone shook their heads. Brooklyn cleared her throat and moved towards Fayebelle, holding out her hand.

"Hi I'm Brooklyn, this is Jia, Audrey and you've met Lola and Harper." She introduced each one and Fayebelle stared at Brooklyn's hand, not taking the offering. Brooklyn waited a beat before lowering her hand awkwardly.

"So…" Brooklyn began glancing around at the others as Fayebelle folded her arms over her chest and raised an eyebrow.

"This is awkward." Audrey piped up, causing Jia to giggle followed by a spluttering cough when Harper and Lola glared at her. Brooklyn inhaled and ran her fingers over her lips, thinking hard.

"What could I do? What can I do?" she thought to herself. She looked around the room, Jia happily oblivious, Audrey focused on dancing, Lola bored, Harper and Fayebelle at opposite ends of the store. She sighed, she wasn't used to this. She thought back to being in her room, sitting and reading or watching tv by herself until her siblings would drag her out of her solitude.

"How about we all go to the mineshaft? Maybe we could find a gem that hasn't found someone? Or maybe we can get an idea of where the umbras and Cato come from?" Brooklyn babbled her suggestions, and the girls stared at her for a long moment.

"Sounds good." Harper said finally, Lola nodded and Fayebelle gave a small shrug of her shoulders and Jia bounded to the door.

"Let's go people!" she cheered and the girls slowly followed her out.

They made it to the docks, the sun was low in the sky, a gentle breeze floating along the waves as few brave people ran in and out of the cold water with couples walking the stretch of the beach hand in hand, The beach was quiet, but a few people were making the most of the rare sunny winter day.

"Okay, where to?" Jia asked. Audrey took off her shoes and wiggled her toes in the sand as Lola lowered her sunglasses onto her nose. Brooklyn looked around and her eyes caught on to the silver mines.

"We should probably start there?" she said, not sounding so sure of herself now. Harper and Fayebelle shook their heads.

"It's too busy."

"We can't access it with everyone around."

They stopped and glared at each other before looking away. Jia pursed her lips together and nudged Brooklyn.

"Oh right… is there a back way in?" she asked. Lola turned to Brooklyn and answered

"No." and pointed to the opening. "It's just that." she added, Brooklyn sighed and ran her fingers through her hair before leaning forward, collecting her hair into one hand and putting a hair band into it. She stood up tall, her hair sitting in a messy bun on top of her head.

"Alright. New plan…" The girls stared at her expectantly whilst Brooklyn stared blankly into space. "Let's. Just. Go." Brooklyn felt her cheeks redden and her heart beginning to race. She hated this greatly, she felt uncomfortable and wanted the ground to swallow her up. She wasn't a leader. Jia gave her a thumbs up and Audrey smiled widely as the other three rolled their eyes in sync. "Ah! We can find another member together! There's a few people here." She breathed out and the group nodded, some more enthusiastic than others. They began walking along the beach together, Audrey patted Brooklyn's shoulder as she and Jia ran off ahead. Lola glanced at the ground and bent down, her fingers trailing over a shiny object and she clicked her fingers. Brooklyn turned, bending down with her. Lola pointed to it and Brooklyn pushed away the sand and picked it up.

"It's just a piece of glass." Lola quipped until Brooklyn let out a small yelp and held it at a distance. Fayebelle let out a bored sigh and headed away from the group.

"Where are you going?" Harper called after her, Fayebelle turned back slightly and stopped.

"We'd cover more ground away from each other." she answered. Harper sneered.

"Fine!"

"Whatever!" Fayebelle whipped around and stomped off. Brooklyn and Lola were busy collecting glass and removing it from the sand, whilst Jia and Audrey were spying on other beach goers, looking for marks.

A little while later, Fayebelle had made her way to the edge of the dock, where it was quiet and away from the others. She stared out at the sea and folded her arms. This was pointless.

"Why aren't you helping?" Harper asked. Fayebelle turned to the purple haired girl who had quietly appeared behind her.

"Because they're currently finding glass. The other two are looking for gems that won't be found, that's clearly not how it works." she answered. Harper stepped closer and Fayebelle lowered her arms and likewise stepped closer to Harper.

"You could still be using this time to get to know them." Harper said, pointing to the girls. Fayebelle let out a laugh.

"Then what's your excuse?" They stepped closer, "Don't think I have forgotten what you said to me, Harper." Fayebelle put both hands on Harper's upper body and shoved her back. Harper's eyes widened before she lunged forward, grabbing Fayebelle.

Jia and Audrey stopped suddenly and turned to the dock, they shared a quick glance before racing over. Brooklyn glanced up from the sand and watched the two running. She followed where they were going and spotted Fayebelle and Harper in each other's faces.

"For crying out loud." she muttered, tapping Lola on the shoulder, who was staring at a pink shell.

"Come on, we gotta stop them." she insisted. Lola glanced up and sighed. The two hurried after Jia and Audrey as Fayebelle shoved Harper again.

"Stop fighting!" Brooklyn yelled. She ran forward as the two were locked together. Brooklyn tried to pull them apart when Harper shoved Fayebelle harder, but Fayebelle let go of Harper and stumbled back into Brooklyn. Brooklyn let out a squeal as her foot caught on the slat and she tumbled backwards into the water.

"Brooklyn!" Jia and Audrey yelled, they ran forward, pushing through Harper and Fayebelle and dropped to their knees searching the water. Lola stared at Harper and Fayebelle her eyes blazing with anger.

"Can you two quit it." She hissed out, the two flinched and turned to the water.

Brooklyn opened her eyes and stared around the crystal clear water, shaking her head and pushing her arms to the side as she made her way back to the surface. She broke the water's surface and inhaled deeply. Jia let out a cheer,

"She's okay! Help me!" She leant over and Audrey rolled on top of Jia keeping her in place. As Lola leant over holding out her hand, Brooklyn gripped their hands, and they heaved her up onto the docks, her hair dripping droplets and her body trembled with a chill.

"Your hairband's gone." Audrey said unhappily. Brooklyn shrugged.

"It's fine." She glanced up at Fayebelle and Harper and they looked away sheepishly. "I think we can call it a day." she said. Audrey hopped up to her feet whilst Lola helped Brooklyn to hers. The group began to make their way back to Altair, as Brooklyn took off her shoes, socks, and her checkered shirt. Their searching coming to an abrupt stop for the day.

The group begrudgingly headed back to Altair Sweet Shop and walked in. It was still dark inside, no Kumiko. Harper shoved the door open, swinging hard on its hinges. Lola followed quietly behind with Jia holding the door. Fayebelle stopped at the entrance and stared hard at Harper's back.

"You know what? I think I'll leave this for now." Fayebelle said. Harper rolled her eyes and Brooklyn nodded, her fingers absently brushing her wet hair. Audrey shrugged her shoulders and hurried inside.

"Yeah… that's fine." Brooklyn muttered.

"But-" Jia began, however Harper pulled her away from the door leaving Brooklyn with Fayebelle.

"Fayebelle, I know this isn't ideal and we're… when you've had time to think about it all. We'll be here." Brooklyn said. Fayebelle gave a slow nod and turned away.

"Thank you for trying… Brooke." she said softly before walking away from the door.

Chapter 24 Uncertain

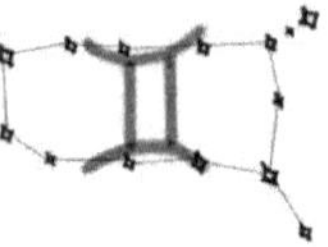

Tai and Xander met up frequently over the next two weeks and both had been left with the task of finding a new member, as the girls were on less civil terms. This time their search had led them to the quiet outskirts of Silver Valley. There had been reports in the news of strange findings and things disappearing, all clearly heading to one place each and every day. The shrine of Aterika.

"So does this place have a special meaning?" Tai asked walking around the area stopping at the cherry blossom tress that created an archway towards the blue and silver shrine.

"For someone who has lived here all their life, your lack of local knowledge is astounding, Tai." Tai chuckled and raked his fingers through his hair.

"You gonna tell me?" He urged. Xander slowly glanced at Tai and took a long slurp of his drink through a straw, Tai raised his eyebrows.

"It keeps evil spirits away, anyone unworthy will disappear forever."

Tai's eyes widened and he pointed at Xander.

"How did you do that?" he exclaimed. Xander let go of his straw and replied

"I did not."

"I did!" They turned around to see a little girl grinning, Tai jumped back and Xander put his drink into his holster. The girl tilted her head to the side and the boys blinked, neither saying a word. The girl took a step forward and the two boys took a corresponding step back.

"The legend says that when the moon is full, with a purple hue, that's when everyone must pass through the gate and those worthy are sent to the stars and those unworthy are left behind." She tilted her head to the side, her eyes were round, circled with dark long eyelashes, her hair pulled into two pigtails, with purple ribbons, and ringlets hanging low.

"Have you been through it?" Xander asked. The little girl chewed on her lower lip.

"I haven't tried."

"I guess we're going to go through it then." Tai said, Xander nodding.

"Thank you. You should probably go home…?"

"Apple."

The two boys raised their eyebrows.

"Sorry, what?"

"My name is Apple." She said grinning, her cheeks dusted with a pink hue. Xander nodded.

"Well…"

"I can come with you." She turned on her heels and began walking ahead, the two boys exchanged looks before they quietly followed the little girl. The walk wasn't long, but the silence dragged. The little girl looked left, then right, then up before pointing forward.

"We're getting close." she said. The two followed her finger and in front of them were stairs on either side of which were draping willow trees with cherry blossom trees dotted along. There were no streetlights, but four spaced out lanterns, swinging slowly. Tai and Xander took a step onto the first step when a howl resonated in the distance.

"I'd like to leave now." Tai laughed, as they followed the little girl up the steps, the wind picking up with each step they took. The clouds were rolling in overhead and the moonlight began to fade as the clouds blocked its path. The lanterns barely let off light.

"Why did we choose to come at night?" Tai asked. Xander gave him a shrug of his shoulders before he answered.

"I had school." he said, deadpan. Tai frowned.

"But you don't go to school?"

"I do… I study at the university."

"Oh. I guess we never actually asked." Tai muttered, suddenly realizing that he didn't know much about any of the team. The little girl bounded along happily, humming to herself as she bounced up the last flight of stairs.

"Hey Xander?"

A small sigh, "Yes Tai?"

"Did you want to… hang out this weekend? Go to the arcade?" he asked. Xander looked at Tai, puzzled. A scraping and tearing sound snapped them from their talk and they looked up to see Apple turn slightly towards the tree line.

"Hey look out!" Tai yelled, the little girl's eyes widened in horror. Xander threw out his whip and it latched around the tree, slowing it down as Tai skidded underneath, grabbing the little girl and pulling her out of the way before the tree hit into the ground and rolled down the steps. Xander pulled back his whip and it disappeared in a puff of sparkles. The girl stared between the two, her eyes full of wonder.

"That was something!" she breathed. The two watched as the trees in front of them began to flicker in and out of existence.

"How far is the archway?" Tai asked. Xander stared at the little girl and cleared his throat. Apple jumped up and turned to them.

"Just over there." She hurried up the steps as the boys followed quickly, the path widening out and the trees now spreading apart, leaving a clear opening to the archway of Aterika, the shrine just beyond.

The two turned around and took a few steps before realizing Apple was no longer with them, they glanced around, their eyes searching for her. Tai and Xander frowned.

"Apple?" Tai called. Xander pointed towards a willow tree.

"Hey… are you okay?" Tai asked, bending down. The girl tilted her head to the side and took a step away.

"I was told not to talk to strangers." she answered. Xander crossed his arms over his chest as Tai held out his hand.

"We just saved you… we're friends right?" he added. The little girl shook her head slowly, before she opened her mouth and let out a scream before running off. Tai and Xander's eyes widened, and they glanced at each other.

"I think we should leave." Tai shuddered, "There is something evil here." And the two turned around and began heading towards the archway. Tai stopped in front of it and stared up at the sign.

"Okay, is this some sort of umbra?" Tai asked, his body tensing.

"Hey!" Xander yelled, the girl turned her head and she smiled

"Hey Tai, hey Xander! Hurry up!" She waved at them; she was already through the archway. Tai glanced at Xander who was staring, mouth agape at the little girl.

"You just ran away from us, screaming." he said. Apple gave him a look.

"Nope. I ran through the archway! Look nothing happened!" she said as she continued down towards the shrine. Tai glanced around, when he spotted Apple poking her head around the tree.

"You're there!" he exclaimed, turning around as he felt Xander's hand on his shoulder. Apple was still in front moving towards the shrine.

"What?" Tai felt his whole-body shiver. He turned back to the willow tree, she was gone. Tai's hand slowly went to his wristband. Apple turned to them and tilted her head to the side her hair draping over her shoulder.

"What's wrong?"

"Boo!"

Apple let out a scream as a hand grabbed her hair and pulled her up. Tai and Xander ran towards her struggling body.

"Let go of her!" Tai yelled. Mala grinned and swung Apple side to side as the poor girl tried to claw at Mala's hand. Xander swung his whip and it slashed across Mala's chest causing her to let go of Apple. Tai ran forward as Apple landed with a thud on her knees and she crawled quickly towards him. He reached out and picked her up, holding her tightly against his chest, her body shaking with tears streaming down her face. Mala turned her attention to Xander and flexed her fingers.

"Back off Scorpio. I want the gem."

"She does not have a gem." Xander said. Mala ran her finger over her chest and noticed a wet substance oozing from her skin. She lifted her hand and tutted.

"You've been a bad boy Scorpio, cutting me like that. I thought you were all so good and pure." She mused, before lowering to all fours.

"Run!" Tai yelled. The two took off and headed back for the stairs as Mala began to chase them, as they stumbled their way down the stairs, Apple scrambled out of Tai's arms, taking his hand, and dragging him into the trees.

"This way!" she yelled at them beckoning them to follow, they kept running until they could no longer hear Mala's screeches. Their breathing heavy, they stayed tucked behind the bushes, as Apple went behind a tree, curled up small and once Tai knew she wasn't moving he turned back to Xander.

"What do we do?" he asked. Xander adjusted his lopsided glasses and took a big gulp of his drink and held it out for Tai who declined, grimacing slightly.

"I think… wait a second!" He leant up over the bushes, his eyes on Mala who was cackling as she dragged Apple back, the little girl in her hands crying.

"They left you! Ha, what monsters they are!" she squealed. Xander leapt from his spot and Tai frowned, glanced behind the tree and gasped. Apple was there, hands covering her ears! He crouched to her and pulled her hands down, she opened her eyes, fear evident.

"Apple. What are you?" he asked. They heard the screams of the little girl and Apple stood up frantically searching before she ran out from her hiding place. Tai jumped up and followed her towards where Xander was. Xander had his whip holding onto the little girl's arm, trying to pull her from Mala, who was hissing and growling at him until her eyes fell upon Tai and Apple. Her grip lessened, Xander's opportunity to save the girl open, and as he pulled with all his strength, she flew forward into Xander's arms.

"There's two?" Mala gaped. Apple ran forward her arms outstretched as her dopple-ganger began to cry harder. Xander let go and Apple hugged the other Apple tightly.

"Berry! I thought you were dead!" Apple wailed; Tai stopped suddenly next to Xander.

"I was so scared Apple." Berry whimpered back. Apple turned to Tai and Xander.

"Please help!" she pleaded. Tai and Xander took the small girls by the hand and began running as Mala let out an angry howl.

"What trickery is this!?"

"They're twins!" Tai exclaimed, Xander nodded. "So that must mean…"

"They are Gemini." Xander confirmed with a proud smile on his face, as the four of them ran back up the steps towards the shrine.

Tai put away his phone and they came to a stop in front of the shrine.

"We can't outrun her, but we can buy some time before the others arrive." he said. Xander agreed. The twins stood behind Xander and Tai as they waited for Mala. Xander turned to the twins.

"Did you two happen to find something like this?" he asked holding out his wrist. Berry hid her face in her sister's back and Apple ran her fingers across the gem.

"Yeah! It was half and half!" she explained, diving into her pocket and holding out a darker purple gem compared to Jia's. "Berry, show them. Berry! They're friends!" Apple said touching her sister on the head a few times until she looked up. She stared at the two of them before pulling out the other half of the gem.

"So, they are one." A voice piped up from above them, perched on the archway was Mala. "How annoying you showed up." She huffed, her tail flicked and twitched. "I suppose I'll have to kill you all now and get the gems."

"Xander! Tai!" Brooklyn's voice suddenly rang out from down the steps, Tai span to face her as Xander pulled Apple and Berry by the hand. Brooklyn came in to view with the others close behind.

"Hey guys!" Tai yelled. Harper and Lola moved towards Xander as he pushed the twins behind him. Allister frowned at Mala whilst Jia, Brooklyn, Fayebelle and Audrey stood next to Tai.

"You've collected more I see." Mala mused. She began to wriggle her fingers and slowly crouched down. The ooze began to drip from her fingers and pools of black and red swirled beneath her as the glowing eyes of the umbras began to appear through the ooze.

Mala stared gleefully at Apple and Berry, both cowering behind Xander who stared blankly at Mala. Brooklyn and Lola stared at the two kids behind Xander and Xander held out his hands.

"Xander?" Harper began, however Tai held up his hand.

"It's alright guys. We've got this." he said, taking a step next to Xander.

"Shall we begin?" Mala asked. Xander did not respond. The two girls shut their eyes and gripped Xander's pant leg. Mala pulled back her mouth.

"What an easy kill they'll be, cowering like fools!" she gurgled. Xander raised his hand, his arm beginning to glow.

"They are just kids." he snarled before swinging his whip at Mala who jumped back behind the creature. She snorted, pointing forward causing the creature to let out an ear-piercing shriek before flying forward.

"Xander!" Apple and Berry yelled before running forward; the two girls held out their arms and in a flurry of light a giant hammer and a giant axe, double the size of the girls, appeared. Xander blinked as Tai and Brooklyn ran to either side, helping him to his feet.

"So, who gave them battle axes and hammers?" Tai laughed. Apple roared loudly in excitement and ran forward.

"I'mma get you demon!" she squealed excitedly as Berry ran after her twin swinging her giant axe side to side.

"Oh, we're so screwed." Brooklyn mused as Xander nodded.

"Thank you Xander." Apple and Berry said together. Harper rolled her shoulders back as Lola sighed, tying her hair up in a ponytail.

"You know, I'm never going to get used to this." she said. Brooklyn gave her a push forward as they all began to leave the shrine, Allister leading the way and chuckling.

"Though, you have to admit it's been pretty fun."

"I think your definition of fun, is something entirely different to what it actually means." Jia remarked. The group laughed and Apple and Berry stopped looking back at the archway.

"Hey, Tai, Xander?" Berry began; the two of them looked down at the twins. "If we're still here with the demons, does that mean we're not worthy?" she asked. The group exchanged glances, however Tai bent down placing a hand on her head.

"Maybe we aren't worthy yet." he said, giving them a grin. Apple nodded and took Xander's hand as they all headed back to the safety of Silver Valley.

Xander sighed, opened the door and walked in. After another late night battle, he was exhausted.

"Why are you out late?" a voice called from the kitchen.

"I was busy." he responded, silence followed before his brother stepped into the doorway. He had blonde hair and a square pair of glasses, in opposition to Xander's.

"I see our parents are out for dinner." he said softly. Xander began making his way to the stairs when his brother cleared his throat.

"Can you explain this?"

Xander stopped and turned his head slightly to see his brother holding up a photo. He stepped down the step.

"Where did you get that?" he demanded, his brother not responding, waiting for a proper answer from Xander. "Cole, where did you get that photo?"

"Answer me first. What are you hiding?" Cole stepped forward, his hand reaching out with the photo. Xander took it from his brother and stared at it.

"This is bigger than you can understand." he answered. Cole folded his arms over his chest.

"You've been disappearing for months now, off on your own. I know our parents don't seem to care but I want to know. Little brother." Cole said.

"How did you find out?" Xander asked again, watching as Cole reached into his pocket.

"It was easy, after finding one of these. It would appear to glow when those people would show up." he said. He held up an aquamarine gem, which glowed brighter every step Cole took towards his brother. "Seems you have one too." Cole gave a short smile as Xander raised his wrist. The glowing gem beaming on his wristband, he stared down at it before looking up at his brother.

"Are you ready to tell me all about it?" Cole asked gesturing to the kitchen table, where a meal and drinks were waiting.

Meanwhile Harper had sat down on her bed, her legs crossed as she stared at her ceiling, her sister already asleep in the adjoining bed. There was a light knock on the door and Harper's sister rolled over groaning. Harper glanced over and her older sister was standing in the doorway.

"I wanted to talk to you about something. Where have you been disappearing to?" she asked. Harper shook her head.

"Nowhere Stella." she answered. Stella raised an eyebrow and gestured for her sister to follow her. Harper exhaled heavily and followed quickly making sure not to wake her younger sister. Harper closed the door behind her and then turned to her sister, folding her arms over her chest.

"Stella, nothing's wrong. If you should worry about anyone you should worry about Klara." she huffed.

"You don't need to be so defensive. I just wanted to know why you haven't looked closer to home?" Stella said cryptically. Harper pushed her hair behind her ear.

"Stel, I need to go to sleep. I really don't know what you're talking about."

"Harper, I just wanted to know when you were going to see that I'm the same." Stella said, Harper had reached for the handle when she saw a glowing light behind her. She turned around and her eyes widened. Stella was holding a gem, and it glowed brightly.

"Can you explain this to me?" she asked quietly.

Harper ran down the street, she couldn't stand being around her sister. After their talk Harper wasn't in the mood to stick around. Harper felt the rain splashing against her face, still running fast until she rounded a corner and ran straight into someone, stumbling back until a hand reached out and grabbed her, keeping her from falling to the ground. She opened her eyes and they widened.

"Xander!" She blinked and saw he wore the same shocked expression that slowly turned to the same worried expression that she wore.

"What are you doing out at one in the morning?" he asked. Harper pulled her wrist out of Xander's hand.

"I found another member." she responded. Xander took his glasses off and wiped them.

"How strange, I have too." he replied, glancing up at the sky. "Maybe we should go somewhere less wet?" he said, his eyes traveling back down to Harper, who nodded.

The two had stopped underneath a tram shelter, both staring bleakly at the night sky filled with clouds and rain, the only light coming from the streetlamp.

"So your sister is one of us too?"

"And your brother?"

"Yes." Xander answered softly, Harper nodded, standing up and moved towards the edge of the shelter, sticking her hand out into the rain, which splashed cold against her palm. Xander watched her quietly, as she chewed on her bottom lip and curled her palm around the raindrops. She turned her head to Xander.

"Why did it have to be them?" she asked, no intention of wanting an answer from Xander as she looked back up at the bleak and dreary sky. Xander adjusted his glasses and Harper shivered.

"Maybe we should head home. You need to get warm." He offered. She nodded and they both stepped out into the rain, their hair and clothes slowly sticking to them as the rain consumed the pair. They took a few steps down the street before all the lights went out. Harper stilled and Xander frowned.

"Like Halloween..." he muttered. Harper blinked fast and jumped to the side, yanking Xander with her.

"Surprise!" Cato yelled, as something jumped at the pair. Xander and Harper growled in unison, as they hit the wall, narrowly escaping Cato's attack.

"Miss me?" he asked grinning as he leant against the wall, his hand running through his hair as he tilted his head. Harper felt Xander's hand grip her wrist giving it a light squeeze before his other hand glowed, Cato jumped back as the whip cracked between them. Xander took off, pulling Harper with him. Cato rolled his eyes and began walking after them, hands in his pockets as he followed.

Harper and Xander pushed open the park gate and ran into the middle, Harper quickly got out her phone and dialed Brooklyn. After a few rings, a begrudged Brooklyn answer.

"Why so early?" she asked bleary.

"It's Cato, he's here at the park." Harper answered quickly. She heard a loud thud and heavy breathing.

"I'm on my way!" Brooklyn exclaimed, feeling a sudden jolt of energy. She ended the call with Harper and Xander put his phone down. At the same time, Harper's phone lit up with a notification from their group chat: Xander had sent a message for them to meet at the park as soon as possible.

"Come out to playyy!" They both glanced in the direction of the sing-song voice. Xander and Harper stood back-to-back, ready for him and his monsters.

"Your fear is that you won't be able to protect your sisters." Cato said stepping closer and closer to Harper, as she froze. Cato grinned and jumped forward. Cato's fingers wrapped around Harper's necklace and her eyes widened in panic. His eyes glinted in excitement as he yanked, the strap shattered, and his fingers gripped the gem.

"Gotcha!" he exclaimed as he pulled back from Harper, she scrambled forward trying to grab the gem, that flickered darker as he moved further away.

"Xan- Scorpio!" she yelled. Xander's whip appeared from behind her and wrapped around Cato's wrist, he sneered. The two were in a tug of war, Cato held tightly to the gem as Xander tried to pull Cato's arm closer so he could grab the gem.

"Harper! Xander! We're here!" a voice called out. The three looked towards the gate and the group came barreling through. Cato scoffed and began pulling harder against the whip, dragging Xander closer, with his free hand Cato began reaching forward for Xander's gem. Harper grabbed his arm and pushed back, trying to keep Cato away from Xander.

"He's got the gem!" Jia cried out, as she noticed Cato holding Harper's gem. Everyone went into a panic and raced forward. Cato shook his head, with one final tug he pulled the whip from Xander and flung it at the others, knocking them to the ground. Harper grabbed his hand and began scratching and clawing at his fingers, Cato growled and shoved the two backwards.

"Whatever happens, get the gem!" Tai ordered, everyone yelling in confirmation. Cato started to run, skidding under the slide and taking off towards the see-saw.

"Get back here!" Audrey yelled as she dived across the see-saw. Cato stepped to the side, before ducking as Allister jumped from the tree and landed inches from where Cato stood. Cato growled and felt his claws twitching to come out.

"You're mine!" Fayebelle shouted as her finger clicked and her arrow appeared in a sea of red sparkles and fired. Cato tilted his head to the side as the arrow sliced his cheek. Fayebelle smirked. Allister and Audrey ran forward with a discarded skipping rope and ran around Cato. Fayebelle held up her bow squared at Cato's face.

"Did you get distracted?" she mused. Cato didn't say anything, as he heard the others cheer.

"We've got him." Jia breathed. Cato let out a roar, the ground around him began shaking and the group felt an enormous surge of power. Cato's fingers began moving and Audrey and Allister tightened their grip. Fayebelle's eyes widened, she took aim and fired. Cato ducked forward and gripped the rope, yanking it forward. Allister and Audrey let out a yell as Cato swung them into each other and they banged heads, collapsing to the ground. The rope lessened around Cato and he scowled at Fayebelle, his foot flicked under the end of the rope and with force flung it at her, smacking her straight in the nose forcing her to let out a scream; her bow and arrow disappeared as she brought her fingers up to her sore nose. Cato turned around; his eyes gleaming.

"You're next." He ran forward and Harper, Xander and Jia dodged to the side as he managed to grab Jia's shoulder and pull her back, before throwing her into the swings. Jia let out a yell as she flew over a swing and landed with a thud on her back.

Xander swung his fist and Cato grabbed his hand, he pulled him forward.

"You can't protect them forever." he hissed. Xander frowned, his fingers gripped the gem and he pulled. Cato's eyes widened in surprise as Xander threw the gem backwards. It landed with a clatter to the ground, bouncing towards the tree and as Cato lifted his leg, his foot connected with Xander's chest and sent him flying. He turned around to Harper, who had picked up her gem and tightened her fingers around it. He ran forward and Harper dodged side to side until Cato took a cheap shot and grabbed her hair and yanked her forward. She let out a yell and Cato grabbed her arm and twisted it back,

"I meant what I said; you feel that? The anguish that you'll lose? That you will not save anyone."

Harper struggled against Cato, and shut her eyes, her heartbeat racing and pain running through her arm. His fingers began pulling hers open and Harper let out a yell, until a loud curse and scream was heard above Cato and Harper. Cato glanced up and his eyes widened in surprise as a pair of green boots came crashing down on him, fingers gripping Cato's hair.

"Do. Not. Pull. Harper's hair!" Lola yelled out, Cato let go of Harper as Tai ran into the mêlé pulling Harper by the hand and lead her away as Cato began scratching Lola's legs to get her off. Lola let go and moved away from him. Cato staggered to his feet.

"You'll regret that." He growled.

"Try it." Lola said back, holding her ground as she clocked Brooklyn. Brooklyn ran forward towards the distracted Cato and lunged, her arms wrapped around Cato's waist and she rugby tackled him to the ground.

"Get off me, Brooke!" Cato yelled, shoving at her head. Brooklyn held on as the two wrestled. Lola summoned her polearm and stepped closer once Brooklyn managed to get on top of Cato. Lola placed her polearm near Cato's throat. He glanced up at her.

"You lose." she said. Tai walked up and folded his arms over his chest and Cato rolled his eyes.

"You sure? You're absolutely positive that you've won? That you haven't just made matters worse?" he said. Brooklyn frowned. Cato's hand slipped from Brooklyn's side and his fingers wrapped around the polearm, Lola let out a gasp as he yanked suddenly and hard so Lola crashed into Brooklyn and the two toppled off Cato. Tai jumped into action and ran forward however Cato sprung up to his feet and swung his leg around tripping Tai up, making him crash to the ground.

"You've lost. Look around you," Cato said. Tai glared up at Cato as he gestured around them, Tai following his gesture and felt a pang of guilt. Everyone was hurt; everyone wasn't okay. Cato walked forward, he reached down and pulled Tai up by his collar.

"Tonight, is your last. I win." he said, his eyes glowing brighter in his joy. A bright sudden light came from behind and four people stood, glowing. A pale aquamarine, a flickering pale gold almost yellow and a dark indigo swirled around the park. Audrey and Allister opened their eyes whilst Lola and Brooklyn covered theirs as Fayebelle, Harper and Jia glanced at the newcomers.

"That's enough." A voice said from the light. Cato frowned and dropped Tai and turned to the newcomers.

"Who are you?"

"The final members." another voice added. The twins jumped forward, a giant purple axe and hammer in their hands.

"We're getting you, demon." The two said in sync. Cato blinked as realisation struck him.

"All twelve?!" he said. The light faded and the four raced forward, Cato shook his head, his eyes flickering quickly to Brooklyn before he snapped his fingers.

"No." he murmured before disappearing into the shadows. The group all staggered to their feet and made their way to Apple and Berry and the other two. Harper and Xander hesitated at the back.

"Who are you?" Brooklyn asked and the two held up their gems in explanation.

"Stella."

"Cole."

The two pointed to Harper and Xander.

"We're their siblings." Cole and Stella said together.

Chapter 25 Chance

"Well that's cute." Jia giggled as Harper and Xander stared at their older siblings. The group began walking out of the park, day light started to break across the horizon.

"This is a joke right?" Fayebelle said glancing around.

"I think it's sweet." Brooklyn said, as Harper sighed.

"I suppose. It's fine." Harper said, Stella smiled and placed her hand on Harper's cheek as she placed her other hand on Apple's head.

"We are a team." She smiled and Cole sighed and ran his hand through his hair.

"Yeah."

Everyone began talking to one another apart from Xander who was staring intently at his brother.

"Why did it have to be him?" Xander thought, following slowly behind the group as they came to a stop by the beach, and he sat down on the edge of the pavement. Jia, Apple and Berry began running on the beach, picking up and throwing sand, while Lola and Brooklyn walked side by side along the beach.

"Are you okay?" Harper asked sitting down next to Xander as everyone else chatted happily and obliviously.

"We were dangerously close to losing." he murmured. Harper agreed, her fists tightening. Everyone seemed relieved and happy that they had won, but it didn't stop the anxiety building in Xander and Harper's hearts. Cato had been right; they were so close to losing. The sun was rising, and the world began to come alive as they all were caught in their own moment, their own world as the darkness was creeping in slowly, ready to engulf the thirteen.

The next day, Tai had made his way to the swimming pool, after a whole night of fighting he was in desperate need of relaxation. The coolness of the water lapped at Tai as he swam lap after lap, never once stopping until finally his lungs and legs gave out. He slowed to a stop and held on to the ledge of the swimming pool. It had been a hectic few months to say the least. Nothing short of a miracle that they had all survived. He pushed himself off the wall and rolled onto his back, floating in the water with his eyes shut. The swish of water, calming his thoughts.

"I guess we really don't know each other…" He thought back to everything that had happened since the start of the school year.

As he left the pool Tai grabbed his phone and opened the message.

It's time to all finally meet. Altair, 10am.

Chapter 26 Gathered

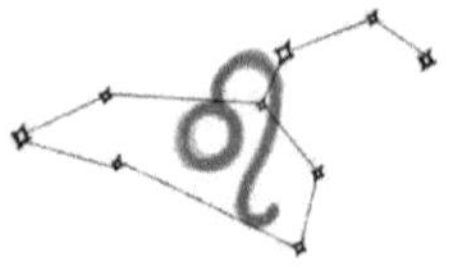

10am arrived and everyone had gathered. "Finally, everyone's here." Kumiko said simply. Brooklyn glanced behind her and there was Harper, Fayebelle and Lola, the trio of not-playing-nice. To the back of the room were Xander, Tai and Allister. Jia and Audrey sat on the counter, Cole and Stella sat around the table and Apple and Berry were bounding around the room taking in all the pretty colours and sweets.

"I'm still not happy about this." Fayebelle said. Audrey snorted.

"You're not happy about anything." she quipped. Fayebelle scowled her response and folded her arms over her chest as the guys groaned a little. Kumiko cleared her throat and headed to the middle of the room.

"Alright let's begin. The twelve of... thirteen of you." She glanced at the twins, and they grinned. "You were all called here by a powerful force, the Queen of our land hopes that you can save our world and your world. It is my job to give you a place and an explanation of what is to come, though you have seen what lies just beyond your simple lives." She raised her hands, and her palms began to glow before she clasped them together and shut her eyes.

Kumiko's hair began to float around her as her body glowed, she threw her arms outwards and sparks flew around her and the whole sweet shop turned dark before stars and galaxies appeared filling the shop.

There was a mixture of excited but calm chatter, though some stayed quiet. Fayebelle was tapping her foot, until it all became too much, and she stood up.

"Enough." she yelled. Everyone stopped and faced her.

"What's wrong now?" Harper huffed, however Fayebelle raised her hand.

"Shut up. I have had just about enough of this. I am not going to be a part of some superhero fantasy." she snapped.

"What do you mean?" Tai asked, walking towards her.

"I don't have time for this… this childish game of make believe." she sneered. Harper rolled her eyes.

"You are such a brat."

"Harper." Stella scolded as Fayebelle walked towards the door. Brooklyn stood up.

"Come on Fayebelle, I know it's unbelievable, but we've all seen it." She was cut off as Fayebelle let out a laugh.

"Grow up." She turned on her heels and walked out the door. The twins jumped to their feet and ran forward.

"Fayebelle." they cried. Fayebelle didn't look back and the door closed quietly behind her.

"You know… I thought L.A. would have broken down like that." Allister said. Lola nodded absently.

"Righ- hey!" She swatted for him, and he ducked causing a few of the others to chuckle. Lola glanced back at the door and folded her arms over her chest. "I didn't even want her as my partner." she sulked, and everyone looked sad once more.

Fayebelle walked along the street, her arms tense and her eyes glued to the ground. She didn't want this, did she? She was struggling to come to terms with this, the fantasy, the magic. She paused as a bell pinged, glanced up, saw a bike roll by and she sighed. She knew Harper would never accept her, nor did she really like the idea of being in Harper's company either.

"Well, if it isn't the Firey red." a voice called from above. Fayebelle looked up to see Cato sat on a bus shelter.

"You really are a glutton for punishment." Fayebelle snapped back. Cato laughed and jumped down.

"Come on… how about we have a truce, you don't like the Zodiacs and neither do I. Why don't we just help each other?" he said walking forwards. Fayebelle stared at him, debating it. She felt the gentle buzz across her neck, Jia had given her a beautiful red velvet necklace to hold her gem and it was flickering. Cato held out his hand.

"You don't have to fight this battle."

Fayebelle lifted her hand when she heard calling from behind her. Tai and the twins were running towards them.

"Don't!" Tai yelled, they stopped behind Fayebelle as Tai stepped in front of her, shielding her from Cato.

"You just love to play hero don't you." Cato said. Tai remained silent and turned to face Fayebelle, his eyes pleading with hers.

"I know this isn't what you wanted. I know you aren't interested in this. But please, we need you." Tai pleaded softly. Fayebelle averted her gaze from Tai. The twins took her hands.

"Please?" Berry said. Tai took a step forward as Cato took three back.

"We're here for you, when you're ready." Tai said. "Applebee to me!" Tai ordered, glaring at the man in front of him, if he could even call him a man. Cato tilted his head to the side and placed a hand on his hip.

"Wouldn't it be better to be alone Aries? Come on, I heard you're one who doesn't need help." he teased. Fayebelle frowned at him as Apple and Berry ran up.

"We're here Tai!" they said in unison. Fayebelle sighed in frustration.

"How does this not bother you Tai?" she asked. Tai stuck his hand out.

"They're my partners, and this is my city." He opened his eyes, and a giant buster sword appeared. He smirked, "Cool." The twins giggled and stood either side of him with their giant axe and giant hammer. "Let's do this Gemini!" And the three ran forward leaving Fayebelle to gawp after them. Cato frowned in dismay.

"I'm not up for fighting you today…" he said and disappeared. Tai, Apple and Berry smiled; their weapons disappeared. They turned to Fayebelle who was standing quietly watching. Tai jogged over to her and placed his hands on her shoulders giving them a squeeze, Fayebelle's eyes flickered to his.

"You're not alone in this. We've got you." he said, tilting his chin towards the twins who grinned happily. Fayebelle pursed her lips together, the gem pulsing warmly.

"Teamwork makes the dream work." Tai mused. Fayebelle snorted at his sarcastic quote and Tai laughed.

"Where did you get that from?" She gave a small smile before shrugging Tai's hands off her shoulders and taking a step back.

"Maybe... it will be okay." She thought, she stared at Tai, Apple and Berry. "Maybe it wouldn't be so bad to join them." She pursed her lips together. "Maybe I can't do this alone." She took a deep breath.

"Alright… I'll help." she said. Tai grinned and the twins let out a small cheer.

"Alright, let's get home guys." Tai said and the four of them headed out. Tai took out his phone and messaged Brooklyn.

She's in.

He waited a moment for her response, listening to the twins talk about themselves to Fayebelle. His phone buzzed.

Thank you x

His smile widened as he put his phone away, this was the start of an epic adventure he thought, as he jogged to catch up to the others.

Weeks had passed and more creatures were showing up, attacking civilians but were stopped by the Zodiacs.

"They're good I'll give them that." Cato mused, resting his chin on his palm, his gaze following Brooklyn. Mala scoffed and twisted her hair around her finger.

"Maybe we're not doing something right." she hissed. Cato sighed and glanced at her.

"What are you talking about?"

"Maybe we need a different approach. Otherwise, mistress won't ever be able to arrive." Mala stood up scanning the area looking for her target.

Chapter 27 Zodiac

Mala stared at the school and slammed her hand into the ground, causing it to crumble and an umbra began to crawl out of the hole.

"Find Capricorn and Virgo. Kill them." she stated, the creatures let out a long screech and galloped into the school. When the screams began, Mala smiled licking her lips as students began running out of the doors, ignoring her they kept running, any direction, fearing for their lives. Mala's grin grew at the excitement. She loved watching people run amid the destruction and chaos as everything falls around them. The total disregard for each other, the nightmares turning into reality.

"Too bad you'll live. My umbras only has one target." she mused. Waiting for the umbra to return with the Zodiacs blood dripping from their teeth.

The roar caused the two girls to stop their experiment. Brooklyn blinked and gripped Lola's hand, as the teacher's eyes widened, and a loud crash came from the next room, students running past screaming. The students around the two began chatting loudly before panicking, the teacher clapped their hands, sweat beading on her brow.

"Calm down, we must leave quietly and calmly." She gestured to the back room, the door between their classroom and the next. Everyone hurried but Lola and Brooklyn held back, watching the door. As a shadow flickered by the door Lola gripped Brooklyn's shoulder and dragged her down as the door to the other classroom shut and the classroom door flung off its hinges.

Lola and Brooklyn leant against the counter.

"This is your fault." Lola whispered, causing Brooklyn to roll her eyes. She slowly leant to the side to peek around the corner.

"If we used our powers, we wouldn't be in this mess." Brooklyn hissed back as they both heard a loud shriek and a thud,

"If we do, we'll be seen on camera." Lola pushed back.

"Then stop complaining. This was the only option." Brooklyn gasped and leant back out of sight as the two umbras emerged from the doorway. Both sniffing the air and growling with each step. Lola shut her eyes as the growling and hissing got louder. Brooklyn shuffled closer to Lola and the two slowly moved further away.

"Is it just me or are these umbras getting more and more intelligent?" she whispered Brooklyn nodded. Brooklyn slowly moved her head to the side as Lola leant closer to her. The creature began sniffing just around the corner. They were evolving. The umbras that Mala and Cato were summoning seemed to be getting more powerful and more cunning. They weren't merely existing; they were thriving.

"Run." Lola hissed, and the two scrambled away as the creature let out a screech and jumped to where the girls were previously. Lola and Brooklyn moved quickly down the aisle as the umbra rose on its hindlegs. Brooklyn spotted the window, and nudged Lola.

"Ready?"

"I don't like this idea."

"Go." The two sprung to their feet and made a dash for the window, Brooklyn picking up a chair as she moved and was ready to throw the chair when the window shattered. Lola frowned,

"Why did it break?" Lola asked. Brooklyn dropped the chair and turned to Lola.

"We don't have time to figure that out, now go!" she said and shoved Lola out of it.

"BROOKLYN!" Lola screamed, Lola shut her eyes but her body landed heavy against another.

"Hey Lola," Allister laughed holding Lola in his arms as Tai held Brooklyn, the two never hit the ground as the two guys were stood at the bottom. The umbra screeched from above and jumped out the window, the boys taking a step back and lowered the girls to the ground.

"You both need to get out of here; we'll deal with this." Tai instructed, Lola nodded, grabbing Brooklyn, they ran off.

"Alright let's do this." Allister said and their fight began. The two umbras let out an ear-piercing scream causing them to flinch.

"You ready for this?" Tai asked. Nodding Allister slipped his foot under an abandoned hockey stick.

"I could really do with an actual weapon." he muttered to himself,

"At least it's not bin lids." Tai said as the two ran forward, the umbra scrambling towards them.

Over in the dance studio Audrey was prancing around the room with Jia drawing her when they heard the screaming. Audrey stopped dancing and headed to the window, leaning over, her head knocking into the window glass. She winced slightly and scanned the area, spotting people running from the science block.

"Damn." she said. Jia left her art book and ran over, her finger pointing to two students flying from a window.

"We need to help!" she gasped as she spotted two glowing figures.

"I know those brown and yellow outfits anywhere. Tai and Allister are already there." she said, taking Jia by the hand. They shuffled into the corner, glancing around, making sure the coast was clear.

"In the middle of twilight make our powers shine." they whispered, their fingers tracing over their gems. The glow began and both girls were swallowed by bright orange and violet lights. Once the lights faded, Audrey ran for the door,

"Let's go!" she yelled, and the two ran out of the building heading for the others.

Stella was sitting at her desk, the radio quietly murmuring next to her, her fingers typing quickly across the keyboard when the news report blasted suddenly.

"There have been numerous calls about an explosion at the Silver Valley school. Officials are saying there was a burst gas pipe in the science department. Our two top reporters, Jack and Dalian will be heading there soon to get you all the facts."

Stella slowed her typing, and her phone began to buzz. She quickly answered and began to gather her things, heading out of the office door.

"You heard right?"

"Yes. I'm on my way there now."

"Just don't get caught." Cole sighed on the other end; she nodded to herself.

"I know. You too." They hung up their call and Stella was in her car, speeding through the empty streets, heading straight to the school, as she transformed.

Cole was walking urgently from his house, when he spotted two bouncy children running towards him.

"Cole."

"Did you hear."

"We gotta help!"

Cole raised his hand silencing the twins, and they snapped their mouths shut.

"Yes. Now." He glanced down an alleyway. "Come on, we need to transform. They're sending reporters." he announced. The twins followed.

"In the middle of twilight make our powers shine." the two girls babbled excitedly whilst Cole closed his eyes and whispered softly to himself. The trio were engulfed in a beautiful display of indigo and aquamarine sparkles.

"We're ready Cole!" the twins said. Cole opened his eyes, the power coursing through his veins, his eyes flickering brighter.

"Let's go." he said, the three quickly making their way out of the alleyway.

Fayebelle was leant against the bar, her hair covering half her face as she read her book, every so often stopping and writing notes in her burgundy gold trimmed book. She placed her rose gold, diamond ended pen down and picked up her espresso and took a small sip.

"Shouldn't you be in school today?" a voice said from behind her. Fayebelle placed her drink down and flicked her wrist.

"It's fine." she answered. She heard a chair scrape, and she turned her attention to Oliver his grey eyes always having that cheeky glint to it. He rested his chin on his elbow and tilted his head slightly, his dazzling smile enchanting her for a moment before his stupid mouth opened.

"You sure about that? Won't your mother be angry."

"Her majesty, doesn't even follow up with the school." Fayebelle answered curtly and went back to her notes, absently drawing swirls in the corners. Oliver let out a troubled sigh, her eyes flickered to him, and she watched as his knuckle on his knee whitened.

"Fayebelle." he hesitated as she leant forward, a smirk gracing her features.

"Oliver?" she replied. She watched his adam's apple bob.

"You-" A siren filled the grand hall and Fayebelle leant back abruptly her plans fizzing away, as she glanced at the glass doors, an ambulance raced by. Fayebelle hopped off her seat, her heels clacking sharply on the marble floor. Oliver frowned and reached for her, but she was gone, running through the open doors, she dialed a number and within a few rings Brooklyn picked up.

"We're in trouble."

"I'm on my way." Fayebelle hung up her phone and kept running, "feet don't fail me now." She muttered to herself, quickening her pace and ignoring the yells coming from Oliver.

Harper pushed another student into a closet.

"Don't come out until the coast is completely clear." she ordered, the two students holding onto each other nodding.

"Where are you going?" one asked. Harper shook her head.

"I need to check on the others, see if there is anyone else. Don't worry I'll be fine." she explained quickly. The two girls went silent as a loud roar came from the adjacent building.

"I'll be back." Harper closed the door and headed away from the closet. She hurried to the corner and tapped her gem. It glowed brightly and she transformed. She ran down another corridor her eyes catching her reflection in the mirror. She slowed to a stop and stared; all pink. She ran her fingers through her thicker hair, glossy and shimmering.

"Pink huh?" she murmured to no one in particular. She felt the gem pulse and she snapped to attention. She had work to do. She kept on running hoping to run into the others as she went.

Mala was sat on a bench staring at her work. She was gleefully thrilled by it all, but she was getting restless, why hadn't they brought the Zodiacs to her? With a stretch and a groan, she stood up and stomped her way to where she first let her creatures emerge.

"Yo!"

"Die."

"So thoughtful." Cato said landing next to her and easily falling into the taller woman's stride. "How is it going?"

"Fine. Butt out." she added for good measure. Cato shook his head as a grin slowly appeared on his lips.

"Were they part of your plan?" he queried. Mala's growls turned into unhinged screams. The other Zodiacs had arrived. She turned to Cato her eyes narrowing, "I want them all dead at my feet." she hissed. Cato gestured in front of him.

"Be my guest, this was your stupid idea."

Allister and Tai were shoved back, flying through the air until they landed hard on the ground. The creatures roared in glee, as Tai struggled to his knees. Allister, laying with his snapped hockey stick, groaned slightly and began coughing, the wind completely knocked from him.

"You okay?" Tai asked. Allister held up his thumb.

"Never better." he grimaced. The two watched from where they were as the creature charged at them. The two braced themselves for another hit, when they saw two screaming girls catapulting their way through the air. Jia and Audrey appeared and jumped into the beast, knocking it sideways. Tai and Allister cheered as they ran up next to them. Xander smacked the creature with his whip and Harper threw a large blanket over the creature. Xander pulled the whip around the creature, and they tied it down and swung it away from Jia and Audrey. A few students screamed as the tail of the creature whacked into the building caused part of the building to fall. Stella ran in and held her arms up as Allister grabbed the three students and hauled them out of the way as the debris was knocked to the side by Stella. Fayebelle, Apple and Berry ran up as Cole waited with Lola and Brooklyn.

"Hurry up." he instructed impatiently, glancing around making sure no one could see as the two girls transformed. Once they were ready, they ran to join the others, the creature roaring loudly. Stella stepped forward,

"Okay everyone. We have work to do. This is the plan." she announced, everyone nodded understanding and Brooklyn looked up, her eyes meeting Cato's. He stared down at her, scowling. After a moment he glanced away and Brooklyn felt arms wrap around her shoulders, she turned and smiled up at Stella.

"Ready?" she asked. Brooklyn nodded and Jia held up her hands.

"Wait, wait!" she declared, everyone looked at her, Fayebelle huffed.

"We don't have time for this."

"Can we please say it all together!" Jia said grabbing Brooklyn's hands and cupping them together so she could beg. Allister laughed and Xander adjusted his glasses.

"Really?" Lola said, Jia pouted and Berry and Apple piped up.

"It's gonna be fun!" they said in unison.

"Alright, just this once." Stella said. Everyone raised their wristbands and said in unison.

"In the middle of twilight, the stars align, make our powers shine!" This time, the sky was lit up with all colours of the rainbow. The gems glowed so bright the warmth it carried caused Cato and Mala to cover their eyes and take a step back as the whole area was covered in glittery lights and colours, each magnificent as it filled the sky. One by one the light faded leaving all thirteen Zodiacs rejuvenated and even brighter than before. Jia let out a squeal as she turned to everyone.

"This is amazing!" she said, the gems on their necklaces all glowing brighter than ever.

"We can gush about it all later Jia." Audrey said laughing, as Apple and Berry twirled around before grabbing Tai's hands.

"Alright, we're splitting up. Tai, Applebee, Xander and Jia, monster one! Do not let it trash anymore of the school." Stella instructed.

"Myself, Cole, Lola and Fayebelle, monster two and keeping civilians safe. We do not want it going anywhere near the city." she said, the groups nodded, and she turned to the final group.

"Finally, Brooklyn, Audrey, Harper and Allister you can handle Cato and Mala."

Tai placed his hand on Brooklyn's shoulder.

"Stay safe alright." he said, she nodded, and the group split up.

"That is one big grizzly bear." Jia said. Xander placed his hand on her shoulder.

"We have got this."

The beast roared and everyone stood ready to fight. It flung itself forward and swatted a big paw at the twins. The two let out a cry, their giant axe and hammer appeared in their hands, above their heads stopping the paw. The two groaned as the bear growled, baring down on them.

"It's too heavy!" they cried, their feet sinking into the ground with each crack of the pavement. Tai jumped forward and slashed his sword against the creature's back, it rose up and Jia ran forward grabbing the twins and pulling them out of harm's way. Xander flicked his wrist, his whip sparkled to life and slashed across the rampaging creature. It let out a howl as Apple and Berry flung their arms out, a bright indigo light flickered in their palms until the great axe and hammer appeared again . Jia placed her hands on her hips and pouted.

"When do I get a cool weapon?" she whined. Xander jumped back away from the monster and frowned at Jia.

"Now is not the time." he insisted. Jia huffed and ran forward, the beast following her.

"I know but I want to have words with the glowing light. I find it unfair!" She yelled over her shoulder as she dived to the side, Tai hopped in front of her, swinging the buster sword towards the umbra, slamming into it flinging it sideways. The five of them let out a quick victory cheer, before noticing the umbra had rolled over and as it lowered its head the spikes on its back grew.

"Oh no." Jia whimpered. The beast let out an earsplitting roar, the twins covering their ears as Xander and Tai ran forward at the creature, coordinating their attack.

Chapter 28 End of a Beginning

"Cole…" Stella began, he glanced back at her and nodded. Lola and Fayebelle jumped up into the air, their arms outstretched. The polearm sprung into shimmering life as the bow and arrow sparkled into an outline before an arrow fired from it and materialized piercing straight into the side of the monster. Lola let out a loud strenuous noise as she flung her polearm into the other side of the umbra. It let out a wail and toppled onto its side, the arrow bedding in deeper.

"They're good." Stella said. Cole stepped up next to her.

Lola circled the fallen umbra, her polearm twirling expertly in her hands. "Hey, ugly!" she called out, her voice a mix of excitement and bravado. "Ready for round two?"

The umbra roared and Fayebelle rolled her eyes.

"Stop antagonizing it." Fayebelle huffed out. The umbra thrashed wildly, its shadowy form twisting and contorting as it tried to dislodge the glittering weapons embedded in its side. Fayebelle notched another shimmering arrow, her face a mask of concentration. The air crackled with energy as she let loose another arrow. It streaked through the air, leaving a trail of sparkling dust as it made contact with the umbra.

"Do we do nothing?" Cole asked. Stella shrugged her shoulders as she watched the green haired girl and the red haired girl make quick work of the umbra. However, it was short lived when the umbra expanded, creating a foreboding shadow. Its teeth became sharper, eyes glimmered with an eerie glow, and its tail twisted and split into two. With a piercing roar its tail whipped around and sliced through Lola's shoulder. She let out a yell and toppled to her knees. Fayebelle whipped around quickly and fired over and over, the arrows sticking in the umbra, but it kept fighting back. Cole sprinted forward, diving for Lola who was cradling her shoulder, as the tail smashed down on the ground narrowly missing the two. They rolled on the floor until they came to a stop. Stella ran towards them as Fayebelle stopped firing. She glanced up.

"Oh." She breathed out as a second tail appeared and slashed through Fayebelle's thigh as she rolled to the side. She let out a painful cry and Cole and Stella stood up facing the umbra.

Cole and Stella exchanged a determined look, their bodies tensing for action. The umbra loomed before them, its twin tails lashing menacingly.

"I guess it's our turn now," Cole said, his voice tight with anticipation.

Stella nodded, her eyes scanning the battlefield. "We need a plan. Fast."

As if on cue, a glint caught Stella's eye. Lola's polearm lay just a few feet away, its magical energy still pulsing faintly.

"Cole, cover me!" Stella shouted as she darted towards the weapon.

The umbra, sensing her movement, whipped one of its tails towards her. Cole leapt into action, grabbing a nearby rock and hurling it at the creature's face. The distraction worked, giving Stella just enough time to snatch up the polearm. She hurled it forward and it stuck in the back of the umbra. Cole glanced up at the building and the tree hanging towards the window. He hurried up it and climbed higher until he was above the umbra and he jumped. With the added power he hurtled down towards the polearm and with his hands he grabbed it, pushing deeper until the ooze gurgled and spluttered all over and through the umbra, pushing until his feet reached the ground. Stella jumped up and down and ran forward as Cole stood up holding the polearm.

"We did it." she exclaimed, Cole nodded a little until he turned to Fayebelle and Lola who were very much worse for wear.

Mala licked her lips and she pointed at Harper.

"I want that one." she grinned, Cato rolling his eyes.

"You have issues." he said pointedly. Allister scoffed.

"I'm here too you know!" he yelled. Mala glanced at him and placed her finger into her mouth and pulled.

"Oh? I didn't even notice you!" she shrieked. The wind around her rose and blasted outwards as her body morphed, and as soon as the wind died down, she launched herself at Harper knocking her backwards, Allister staring in horror.

"Libra!" He disappeared after Mala and Harper.

Harper blocked the fist that slammed into her forearm, she skidded backwards and frowned. Mala grinned and slashed her tail over and over at Harper, slicing across her cheek, thigh, shoulder and stomach. Harper let out a hiss of pain before dropping to her knee, panting heavily, as Mala stood cackling.

"The pain you are in is glorious! Bleed for me pinkie!" she shrieked and lunged. Harper shut her eyes, a moment flickered by and Mala let out a scream toppling sideways with Allister throwing her to the ground. Harper opened her eyes and scrambled to her feet, she raced forward and held out her arms as Mala kicked Allister hard, flinging him into Harper. They were both thrown back, sliding across the ground. Harper grunted as Allister's weight crashed into her, knocking the wind from her lungs. They tumbled across the ground, a tangle of limbs and gasping breaths, Mala's maniacal laughter echoed through the air, sending chills down Harper's spine.

"Two for the price of one!" Mala cackled, her tail whipping back and forth in excitement. "How delightful!"

Allister rolled off Harper, his eyes darting between her and their adversary. "You okay?" he whispered, voice tight with concern. "What do we do?" he asked, Harper's gaze hardened at Mala who was pulling her hair, her face and getting ready to charge at them.

"We… we need to overwhelm her." she panted. Allister frowned. They got to their feet and ran at Mala. Diving and dodging her tail whilst throwing punches and kicks. They kept going, becoming more exhausted as they went, until Harper got a clean kick to Mala's face. Mala's head twisted to the side, she growled and turned back to them, about to dive when a loud roar filled the air, a hammer, and an axe swung through the bear and it toppled on top of Mala. A little cackle coming from the twins as they stared at the fizzing bear. Xander and Tai strolled up, breathing heavily. Harper and Allister let out a sigh of relief and watched as Mala's body grappled through the disappearing umbra.

With a bone-chilling shriek, Mala burst through the dissipating bear, her eyes blazing with fury. Her scales seemed to shimmer and shift, taking on an iridescent quality that hadn't been there before. The ground beneath her feet began to smoke and sizzle, small fissures spreading outward like a spiderweb.

"You haven't seen the last of me." And she was gone. Leaving the group to collapse in exhaustion, waiting for the others.

Cato folded his arms as Audrey stepped in front of Brooklyn.

"Looks like we're the last two left. You ready Cato?" she asked. Cato didn't say anything, his eyes fixed on Brooklyn. Audrey frowned and stepped into his eyeline. His eyes narrowed at her, as Audrey readied herself.

"Fine, I'll destroy you too." he hissed as his body transformed. The two girls stood ready, as Cato charged forward. Brooklyn summoned her ribbon, watching it sparkle to life. She twirled the ribbon around her head, throwing it forward, it wrapped around Cato's arm, he growled, forced to stop. He yanked his arm hard above his head, Brooklyn letting out a gasp as she was hurtled forward. Audrey reached out her hand.

"No!" she yelled. Cato dropped slightly, and Brooklyn toppled over him, the ribbon loosening as her back smacked into the ground. She let out a splutter as Cato ran forward. Audrey jumped back again and again as Cato's claws slashed left and right, Audrey dropped down and spun her leg around. Cato felt her leg hit his shin, and he stumbled. Audrey got up and swung her fist into his cheek. She let out a delighted gasp, and Cato snarled turning his head slowly to her. Audrey's eyes widened as she readied herself, Cato towering over her, menacingly. She swung her leg up and Cato caught it in his claw, she let out a grunt and Cato twisted, swinging her sideways, forcing her to yell out as the pain shot up her leg, she rolled onto the ground hard. Audrey staggered back up, bruises and small cuts scattered on her body. She ran at Cato, he sneered at her, before stepping back and booting her hard in the chest, she cried out as she hurtled back, feeling something crack under the weight of his foot. His hand shot out and he grabbed the necklace, it snapped as Audrey fell and Cato held the gem in his clawed hand.

"Did you really think that just because I had a flair, I wouldn't be strong enough to destroy you?" he gloated. Audrey gasped for air and gripped her painful sides.

"He's got my gem!" Audrey cried. Brooklyn turned around as Cato dashed past her. Audrey tried to get up from the ground but the pain in her ribs made her cry out. Brooklyn gulped and turned between the two. Audrey looked at her, desperation in her eyes.

"Stop him! Brooklyn you have to stop him!" she pleaded. Brooklyn tried to reach for Audrey, but she shook her head vigorously.

"He- he can't take it! He can't win! They- please I'll be fine!" she said. Brooklyn closed her eyes in anguish, took one last look at Audrey before running after Cato, leaving everyone else to continue their fight.

Brooklyn spotted the blue haired boy, as she scanned around, she had to cut him off. She spotted the bridge that led to the beach, she watched as Cato ran down the steps. She weighed her options before she shook her head.

"Sod it." She panted as she ran to the bridge and clambered up onto the railing. She took a deep inhale.

"Take this!" Brooklyn yelled diving off the bridge. Cato glanced up and he de-morphed as a yelp left his lips and she tackled him to the ground. His head hit the ground and he growled as he tried to keep Brooklyn at bay.

"What is wrong with you?" he shouted. Brooklyn struggled as she kept trying to untangle her arms from his hands.

"So much, but I don't have time to go into it right now!" She snapped back. Cato stopped struggling and stared at Brooklyn. Her eyes were like molten silver, swirling with a hint of wildness and passion, a glint of madness that made her seem all the more dangerous and enticing.

"Give it back!" she grunted. Cato gripped her wrists, and she struggled against him. "I won't let you win!" she barked defiantly. Cato let out an annoyed cry and pushed harder against her.

"What would you know about it anyway?" He huffed, his eyes closing against the strain. They had been fighting for too long now and he hadn't the strength to morph again. Brooklyn stared at him, Cato took a deep breath and opened his eyes and Brooklyn immediately stopped struggling, her expression softening as she looked into his piercing green eyes. His tousled blue hair gave him a wild, untamed appearance, but in that moment, he seemed almost human to her. His strong jawline and chiselled features made him both intimidating and alluring at the same time. She couldn't help but be drawn to him despite their current predicament.

"What?"

He opened his eyes and glared at her,

"You heard me," Cato said through gritted teeth. "What would you know about any of this?"

Brooklyn's silver eyes widened, a mix of confusion and frustration swirling in their depths. She stopped struggling against his grip, her breath coming in short pants.

"I... I know enough," she stammered, but the certainty in her voice wavered.

Cato loosened his grip slightly, sensing a shift in the dynamic. "Do you? Or are you just following orders blindly?"

Brooklyn's brow furrowed, and for a moment, doubt flickered across her face. The sound of the others fighting in the distance drifted from afar, a stark contrast to what they were doing.

"I know that we can't let you have our gems." she said, her voice softer now. "I can't let you harm Silver Valley."

Cato let out a laugh and let go of Brooklyn. His fingers opened around the gem and her eyes flickered to it.

"Take it Brooke, I'm bored of this." he said, tempting her. Brooklyn paused and he raised an eyebrow. "Now Brooke." he ordered. she leant toward him, took the gem from his hand and staggered to her feet. She moved away from him.

"Cato." a voice hissed. Mala suddenly appeared behind him, crouching on all fours, her hair dishevelled, and she was no longer in her scary demonic form. Mala yanked Cato into sitting and he glanced back at Mala slightly.

"Let's go. It's done." she said. The two disappeared quickly into the shadows and Brooklyn let out a sigh of relief. She turned to the others, her fingers burning from the gem before she stumbled her way over to Audrey, held out her hand and Audrey shakily reached up and took the gem. Brooklyn moved around before stopping, the exhaustion taking over, hanging her head.

Jia lay on the ground her chest heaving up and down, Audrey was on her knees, her flame-coloured choppy hair was masking her face, her head hanging low. Allister was helping up Lola who gripped her shoulder. Harper and Xander stood next to each other, both staring at the siblings. Tai, Apple and Berry were sitting on the ground, checking over Fayebelle, who sat with her leg elevated on Tai's lap, wincing every so often. Cole straightened out his waistcoat and nodded at Stella who breathed a sigh of relief before placing her hand on Brooklyn's shoulder who was staring blankly into space.

"We did it." she said. Brooklyn glanced back at her; the only warmth she felt was coming from her gem.

"Then why do I feel like we… missed something important?" Brooklyn asked, her eyes flitting to everyone, looking worn out and totally out of their league. "Why does it feel like we lost?" she added. Stella wrapped her arms around the younger girl's neck and squeezed tightly.

"We're all okay, Silver Valley is okay." she answered, "We just weren't prepared for how strong Cato and Mala were. But we did it. We survived." she continued, her voice gentle and calming. Brooklyn inhaled, the whiff of vanilla and strawberries greeted her as Stella's shimmering gold hair tickled her nose. Her shoulders relaxed and she hugged her in return before letting go. A rising noise began to fill the area as groups of people began appearing. Jia craned her head to the side as the crowds talked over one another, surrounding them in a circle.

"The heroes saved our Silver Valley Mall! How will we ever repay them?" a man asked as he walked forward with his camera crew. Tai rocked on his back and kipped up, holding his hand out he pulled Apple and Berry to their feet.

"Is this truly a good thing? Are we in serious trouble? What will the mayor have to say?" another voice piped in, his own set of crew following him. The crowd nodded along, following their every word as the group moved closer together.

"One can only imagine as our quiet city is now home to monsters!"

The group weary and shattered, stumbled together trying to get out of the camera's sight until a voice piped up.

"What have they got to say?" The man moved forward blocking Jia from leaving. Cameras and phones were blocking her path and her eyes widened in fear. "Where have you come from? Look at your outfits!" one voice said as talk began to surround the group. Fayebelle and Lola stepped back as a group of adults started questioning them.

"Why are you here? Do we need to worry now that there are monsters?" another voice asked, turning his attention to Tai and Xander. Jia shook her hands and took a step back as the group were slowly encircled.

"Well?" the other man said, cameras flashed, blinding the group. No one spoke as they tried desperately to gather their thoughts as more and more questions were thrown at them as the crowd seemed to grow with every passing second. Stella stared at Brooklyn who, in turn, stared at the news anchors, Jack and Dalian, handsome and devilish. One wore a dark midnight suit with a striking blood red tie, whilst the other ocean blue and a royal purple tie as alike and as different as they come but the pushiest news anchors around.

"Can you shed any light on this matter?" Jack asked insistently as Dalian pushed the microphone against Stella's mouth.

"Cat got your tongue?" he teased, earning a round of chuckles from his adoring fans. Stella stepped forward and inhaled deeply.

"Everyone, there is no need to worry. We are here to protect this wonderful city from the creatures that threaten it. We vow to keep each and every one of you safe from whatever may come! My team..." She gazed at every single one of the group and gave them all a smile. "We are the Zodiacs, and we will keep the peace. No matter what." She announced. Everyone began talking all at once and Stella gestured to the side, the team making a hasty retreat. A gust of wind blew through the area causing the public to close their eyes and turn their heads as the Zodiacs disappeared, leaving Dalian and Jack to continue to cover the story.

Cato and Mala stared down at the twelve Zodiacs as they walked through the park away from all prying eyes.

"Looks like we failed." Cato muttered. Mala growled and stared down at each of them as they began to walk away from the adoring crowd.

"No. We still have time." she spat back. Cato frowned and watched as Sagittarius put his arm around Capricorn, his teeth gritted together, and he turned away.

"If we don't, he'll show up, and we'll be in trouble with Mistress." Cato hissed. Mala stared after Cato, her hair blowing in the cold breeze as the sun set behind the cliffs. Cato balled his hands, and took one more step, her face flashing in his mind before he disappeared back to the mineshaft, his anger boiling, leaving Mala with the shadows twisting and clawing at her body, until twilights' darkness covered Silver Valley and the Stars began to shine.

End

www.ingramcontent.com/pod-product-compliance
Lightning Source LLC
Chambersburg PA
CBHW041046310726
48978CB00011BA/452